ELENA EVERHART

The Alpha's Forbidden Contract

A Werewolf Romance of Power and Desire

Contents

One

Chapter 1: A Life in Chains

Lyra's fingers ached as she scrubbed the stone floor, her breath misting in the cold morning air. The sun hadn't risen yet, and the packhouse was silent except for the occasional rustle from the sleeping wolves above. She worked in the shadows, unseen and forgotten, a ghost among the living. The dampness of the stones seeped through her threadbare clothing, chilling her to the bone, but she had grown used to the cold—both the physical and emotional kind.

Each morning was the same, and each night blurred into the next. She lived like a machine, moving through the motions of her captivity without thinking. Her wolf was silent, her spirit bound by her brother's cruel magic. Caius had ensured that the wild part of her was locked away, leaving her powerless and broken. Once, she had been someone important—a daughter of Alphas, a girl with a future. Now, she was nothing more than a slave in the home she had once called her own.

A door creaked open, and Lyra stiffened, her heart thudding. Caius's lieutenant, Rourke, stepped into the hallway. He was a massive brute of a man, with scars crisscrossing his face and arms. His boots thudded against the floor, each step sending tremors through her body.

"Get up," Rourke growled, his voice rough as gravel. "Alpha Caius wants the main hall ready for tonight's meeting. And don't think about slacking, girl. You know what happens if you do."

Lyra nodded silently, keeping her eyes on the floor. She didn't need a reminder. The last time she had been late with her tasks, Caius had bound her even tighter, leaving her gasping for breath as her wolf howled inside her mind, desperate for release.

As Rourke disappeared down the hall, Lyra exhaled slowly, pushing herself to her feet. She winced as pain shot through her knees. Her life had become a string of endless tasks, all to keep Caius's packhouse running smoothly while she lived in the shadows. No one looked at her. No one acknowledged her presence. That was the way Caius wanted it. She was an embarrassment, a shameful reminder of the sister he had once protected but now despised.

But something was different today. Caius had mentioned a visitor—someone important. Alpha Damon Darkholme. Even the name sent a shiver down her spine. She had heard whispers about him, stories of his power, his ruthlessness, and his strange, crimson eyes. A dangerous man who had no equal among wolves. Why would he come here, to Blackthorn Hollow?

Lyra didn't know, but something in her gut twisted with unease. She bent down, resuming her work, but the thoughts kept gnawing at her mind. What did Caius want from Damon? And why did she feel as if her life was about to change in ways she couldn't yet understand?

The large oak table in the main hall gleamed under the firelight, each surface polished to perfection by Lyra's hand. The pack gathered around it, their voices a low murmur of anticipation. Caius sat at the head, his sharp eyes surveying the room, his fingers drumming rhythmically on the armrest of his chair. Lyra stood at the far corner of the room, her presence unnoticed as she poured wine into goblets, trying to make herself invisible.

"Damon Darkholme will arrive by nightfall," Caius said, his voice carrying over the quiet. His pack members stilled, their expressions tense. "We will discuss terms of an alliance. I don't need to remind you what's at stake here."

Lyra's hands trembled as she set the goblet in front of Rourke, careful not to spill a drop. The tension in the room was thick, almost suffocating. Caius's wolves were on edge. They feared Damon, even though they hadn't met him. His reputation preceded him—an Alpha who ruled with an iron fist, feared by all who opposed him.

"An alliance with Damon Darkholme?" one of the pack members asked, a note of doubt in his voice. "Do you really think we can trust him?"

Caius's eyes flashed dangerously. "We don't have to trust him. We just need him on our side."

Lyra's heart raced as she moved quietly behind Caius, refilling his goblet. She had seen this look in his eyes before—the look he wore when he was about to make a move that would change everything. He hadn't said what the terms of the contract were, but Lyra sensed something dark in the air, something that made her stomach churn.

Her fingers brushed against the rim of Caius's goblet as she poured the wine, and he turned his head sharply, his cold gaze locking onto hers. "Out," he snapped, his voice like a whip. "You've done enough."

Lyra flinched but nodded quickly, retreating toward the door. As she stepped into the hall, she could still hear Caius's voice carrying through the stone walls. "This deal will secure our future. Darkholme won't refuse. Not once he sees what we have to offer."

The small, drafty room beneath the packhouse felt more like a prison than a home. Lyra closed the door behind her, leaning against it as she let out a shaky breath. Her hands still trembled from the tension in the main hall. She knew something was wrong. Caius had never spoken of an alliance before, and certainly not one with someone like Damon Darkholme.

Her mind wandered back to the night that had changed everything. The night she had lost control. She could still see the terrified look in her mother's eyes as her wolf surged to the surface, as though it had a mind of its own. Her father had tried to reach her, but it was too late. By the time Lyra had regained control, they were gone—both of them. And Caius had never forgiven her.

He had bound her wolf that same night, using ancient magic to lock it away inside her. She hadn't felt its presence in years, hadn't shifted since that fateful night. The binding spell was like a cage, and inside, her wolf raged, trapped and powerless.

Lyra sank onto the small cot in the corner of the room, pulling her knees to her chest. The guilt was always there, gnawing at her insides, a constant reminder of her failure. She deserved this life, she told herself. She deserved the pain, the servitude, the isolation. It was her punishment for what she had done.

But deep down, buried beneath the layers of guilt and shame, there was a spark of defiance. A small, flickering ember that refused to die. Sometimes, late at night, she would dream of running through the forest, her wolf free and wild, untethered by Caius's magic. But dreams were just that—dreams. And reality was far crueler.

A knock on the door jolted her from her thoughts. She stood, brushing her hands on her apron before opening the door a crack. Rourke stood there, his expression unreadable.

"Get upstairs," he grunted. "The Alpha has visitors."

Lyra stood in the shadow of the packhouse as the wind swept through the trees, carrying with it the faint scent of pine and damp earth. The evening sky had darkened to a deep blue, and the first stars began to peek through the clouds. She heard the distant sound of hooves on the ground before she saw them—a group of riders approaching, their cloaks billowing behind them like shadows.

At the front of the group rode Damon Darkholme.

Even from a distance, she could see his powerful frame, the way he held himself with an air of authority that commanded respect. His horse, a massive black stallion, snorted as they drew closer, its hooves kicking up dirt in the fading light.

Lyra's breath hitched in her throat. There was something about him, something that made her wolf stir for the first time in years. She stepped back, retreating further into the shadows, but her eyes never left Damon. His presence was magnetic, impossible to ignore.

As the group came to a halt outside the packhouse, Damon dismounted with a fluid grace that belied his size. His crimson eyes scanned the area, and for a brief moment, they seemed to land on her. Lyra's heart raced as their gazes locked, and she quickly ducked her head, turning away before he could see her.

What was it about him? Why did her wolf react to him, when it had been silent for so long?

Caius stepped forward to greet his guest, his voice smooth and practiced.

5

"Welcome, Alpha Darkholme. We've been expecting you."

The flickering torchlight cast long shadows across the main hall as Caius and Damon sat across from one another at the large oak table. Lyra stood near the doorway, watching from a distance as she refilled goblets, trying to blend into the background. The tension in the room was palpable, an invisible current running between the two Alphas.

Caius leaned back in his chair, a practiced smile on his face. "I trust your journey was uneventful."

Damon's gaze was sharp, his crimson eyes narrowing slightly. "It was. Let's not waste time with pleasantries, Caius. We both know why I'm here."

Caius's smile faltered for a moment, but he quickly recovered. "Of course. Straight to business, then."

Lyra moved quietly around the table, her heart pounding in her chest. She could feel Damon's eyes on her, even though he said nothing. There was something unsettling about the way he watched her, as if he could sense something she didn't even understand herself.

"As I mentioned in my message," Caius continued, "an alliance between our packs would be mutually beneficial. With your strength and my resources, we could dominate the territory."

Damon remained silent for a moment, his eyes flickering briefly toward Lyra before settling back on Caius. "What exactly do you have to offer, Caius?"

Caius's smile widened, but there was a coldness in his eyes. "Let's just say... I have something that might interest you."

Lyra's hands trembled as she poured the wine, her mind racing. What was

Caius planning? And why did she have the sinking feeling that she was about to be caught in the middle of something far darker than she could imagine?

Two

Chapter 2: The Arrival of the Alpha

The packhouse doors creaked open as Damon Darkholme stepped inside, his tall, imposing figure framed by the cold twilight spilling through the doorway. His crimson eyes swept across the room, sharp and unyielding, catching every detail. The pack stilled, the murmurs of conversation dying as soon as they laid eyes on the infamous Alpha. Lyra stood in the shadows near the far wall, frozen as she watched him. Her heart beat faster, her hands trembling. It wasn't just his reputation that unnerved her. It was the way her wolf stirred within her, faint but present, as if reacting to Damon's arrival.

Damon exuded authority. The air itself seemed heavier with his presence, thick with tension as though it recognized the power he carried. Caius rose from his seat at the head of the table, his smile forced but polished, a mask of control. Lyra knew that look. Her brother was already calculating, already playing his angles, hoping to gain Damon's favor.

"Welcome to Blackthorn Hollow, Alpha Darkholme," Caius said, his voice smooth, too smooth. "It's an honor to have you here."

Damon's gaze lingered on Caius for a moment before shifting to survey the rest of the room. His silence spoke volumes, an unspoken challenge that made the tension worse. Lyra ducked her head as Damon's eyes passed over her, but not before feeling the weight of his stare. It was brief, but it made her heart skip. He hadn't truly seen her, but the brief connection left her rattled.

"I don't waste time on pleasantries," Damon said finally, his voice low, carrying the threat of power beneath its calm surface. "Let's get to the matter at hand."

Caius's smile faltered for only a split second before he nodded. "Of course."

As they moved to the main table, Lyra backed away, silently excusing herself from the room. Her hands were shaking now, the strange pull toward Damon leaving her unsettled. He hadn't even noticed her, not really, and yet her wolf stirred at the edge of her consciousness. She could almost feel its presence, faint but undeniable. She hadn't felt her wolf in years—not since Caius had bound it. Now, all because of one man's arrival, the part of her that had been locked away was waking.

Once Lyra had slipped out of the room, the atmosphere inside shifted. Caius motioned for his lieutenants to leave, closing the doors behind them. It was just him and Damon now, the two Alphas facing off at the table.

"We both know why I'm here," Damon said, his fingers tracing the rim of the goblet before him, his gaze steady on Caius. "You've got a problem, and you need my help."

Caius leaned back in his chair, trying to appear casual, but Lyra had seen enough of her brother to recognize his unease. He was nervous, even if he masked it well. Damon's reputation wasn't just talk—he was known for his ruthlessness, for taking what he wanted without hesitation. This alliance wasn't just about strength. It was about survival.

"There are... rival packs," Caius began, choosing his words carefully. "They've been encroaching on our borders for months now. If this continues, it won't be long before Blackthorn Hollow falls. We need a strong partner."

Damon raised an eyebrow, unimpressed. "And what do you have to offer that's worth my protection?"

Caius hesitated. Damon was no fool. A simple alliance wasn't enough. He needed more, something valuable. Caius leaned forward, his smile returning. "I can offer you something rare. Something that no one else can."

Damon's expression didn't change, but his eyes gleamed with interest. "Go on."

Caius kept the details vague, teasing the information out slowly. "I have a unique... asset. One that could be of great interest to you."

Damon's lips twitched in a faint smile. "I'm listening."

Outside, Lyra paced in the shadows, her breath visible in the cool night air. She wrapped her arms around herself, trying to fight the growing anxiety gnawing at her. There was something about Damon Darkholme, something that unsettled her deeply. She couldn't shake the strange pull she felt toward him, as though her wolf recognized him on some level she couldn't yet understand.

But it wasn't just that. It was Caius, too. Her brother had been on edge for weeks now, preparing for this moment. He wanted Damon's alliance badly, but Lyra knew her brother. Caius didn't do anything without a plan, and whatever deal he was striking with Damon, she feared it would involve her.

The thought made her stomach twist. Caius had kept her bound for years, using his position as Alpha to suppress her power, to keep her in the shadows where she wouldn't be a threat to him. But now, with Damon's arrival, Lyra had a sinking feeling that she was part of the bargain. Caius wouldn't hesitate to use her if it meant securing the alliance.

Her wolf stirred again, faint but insistent, pushing against the magical binding that had kept it dormant. Lyra closed her eyes, trying to steady her breathing. For years, she had lived with the weight of her wolf's absence, the silence in her soul a constant reminder of the night she had lost control, the night her parents had died. Caius had bound her after that, caging her wolf in an effort to punish her—and to protect himself from her power.

Now, with Damon so close, her wolf was trying to wake. But what did it mean?

Damon stepped outside, his breath steady as he surveyed the darkened forest surrounding Blackthorn Hollow. The night was quiet, but he could sense something just beneath the surface, something hidden. His crimson eyes scanned the treeline, catching every flicker of movement, every shift in the shadows.

There was an odd energy here, something off-kilter that he couldn't quite place. He'd been in countless territories before, but this one felt... different. There was a tension in the air, not just from the pack's fear of him, but something more. It was subtle, but Damon had learned to trust his instincts. They'd kept him alive this long.

As he breathed in the crisp air, a faint scent teased his senses. It was faint, almost imperceptible, but it lingered, stirring something deep within him. Damon's brow furrowed as he tried to place it. It wasn't the scent of the pack members—it was something else, something elusive. His thoughts flashed to the girl he'd noticed earlier. The one who had slipped away before he could get a closer look. There had been something strange about her, something that didn't fit with the rest of the pack.

He took another breath, letting the scent fill his lungs. It was familiar, but he couldn't place why. His eyes narrowed. Caius was hiding something, and Damon had a feeling it involved that girl.

Damon re-entered the packhouse, his footsteps quiet but purposeful as he approached the main hall. Caius sat at the head of the table, his smile faltering as Damon returned. The tension between the two Alphas was thick, the air practically vibrating with unspoken threats.

Damon sat down slowly, his eyes locked on Caius. "Enough games, Caius. I want the truth."

Caius blinked, feigning confusion. "I've told you the truth, Damon. Our packs stand to gain—"

"No," Damon interrupted, his voice low and dangerous. "I want to know what you're hiding."

Caius swallowed, his hands clenching the arms of his chair. Damon's presence was suffocating, and he knew he couldn't afford to push him too far. But revealing the full truth would mean showing his hand, and he wasn't ready for that yet.

"There's… someone," Caius admitted, choosing his words carefully. "Someone who might be of interest to you."

Damon's eyes gleamed with interest. "Go on."

Caius hesitated, glancing toward the door where Lyra had disappeared moments before. "She's… unique. But I'll need to show you to explain fully."

Lyra, listening from the hallway, felt her heart drop. She knew, without a doubt, that her brother was talking about her. Damon leaned back in his chair, a slow, predatory smile forming on his lips.

"Show me."

Three

Chapter 3: The Crimson Contract

The heavy door groaned as Caius pushed it open, leading Damon into a dimly lit chamber deep within the packhouse. Lyra stood in the corner, her heart racing as her brother's footsteps echoed off the stone walls. She tried to keep her breathing steady, but the tension was unbearable. Damon's presence loomed like a shadow—silent, calculating, and impossible to ignore.

Caius motioned for Damon to enter, and the Alpha stepped forward without hesitation, his crimson eyes locking onto Lyra immediately. She felt the weight of his gaze, a strange mix of curiosity and something else she couldn't quite identify. Fear crawled up her spine, and she instinctively shrank back against the cold wall, though she knew there was no escape.

"This is her," Caius said, his voice low, almost reverent. "My sister, Lyra."

Damon didn't respond at first, his eyes still fixed on her. Lyra felt exposed, as though every secret she had ever kept was being laid bare under his gaze. The silence stretched, thick with unspoken tension, until finally, Damon spoke.

"And what makes her so special?" His voice was calm, but there was a dangerous edge to it, as if he already knew the answer but wanted to hear Caius squirm.

Caius cleared his throat, stepping forward. "She killed our parents," he began, the words heavy with accusation. "Lost control of her wolf and hasn't shifted since. I had to bind her to protect the pack."

Lyra clenched her fists, her nails biting into her palms. The guilt had never left her, but hearing Caius reduce her entire life to that single moment burned deeper than she expected. She glanced up at Damon, who was now watching her with renewed interest.

"But she's powerful," Caius continued. "Her wolf... if released, could rival any Alpha's strength. With the right guidance, she could be of great use to you."

Damon's expression remained unreadable, but his eyes never left Lyra. She swallowed hard, the gravity of her situation settling in her chest like a stone.

Damon moved closer to Lyra, each step deliberate, his eyes narrowing as he studied her. Caius hovered in the background, eager to prove Lyra's worth, but Damon didn't need his words. He could feel the faint pulse of power under the surface—dormant, restrained, but very much alive.

"How long has she been bound?" Damon asked, his voice quiet but commanding.

Lyra's heart pounded in her ears as she tried to find her voice. "Six years," she whispered, barely able to meet his gaze.

Damon tilted his head, curiosity flickering in his eyes. "And why haven't you tried to break free?"

15

Lyra hesitated. No one had ever asked her that before. The truth was tangled in guilt and fear, and the thought of explaining it to this man—this Alpha—was overwhelming. But Damon's gaze was unrelenting, and after a moment, she spoke.

"I… don't know if I can," she admitted, her voice trembling. "The spell is strong. I haven't felt my wolf in years."

Damon stepped even closer, until he was just inches away from her. Lyra held her breath, her pulse quickening. His presence was overwhelming, and for the first time in years, she felt the faint stirrings of her wolf, scratching at the edges of the spell that held it captive.

"You could," Damon said softly, his eyes darkening with something unreadable. "If you wanted to."

Lyra's throat tightened. Wanting freedom and actually taking it were two very different things. And for as much as she longed to be free, there was still a part of her that feared what that freedom might bring.

Caius cleared his throat from across the room, clearly sensing the shift in Damon's focus. "I can transfer control of the binding spell to you," he offered, stepping forward as if trying to regain control of the situation. "Once the spell is yours, you can release her—or keep her bound—however you see fit."

Damon didn't respond right away, his gaze still locked on Lyra. She could feel her brother's words sinking in, each one twisting her insides with dread. Caius spoke of her like she was a tool, something to be wielded by whoever held the key to her cage. And now, that key was being offered to Damon.

"What do you want, Lyra?" Damon's question broke through the tension, his voice softer now, as though he were giving her a choice she'd never had before.

Lyra blinked, taken aback. No one had ever asked her what she wanted. It had always been decided for her—by Caius, by the pack, by the weight of her own guilt. She opened her mouth, but the words stuck in her throat. Freedom? It seemed impossible. And yet…

"She's in no position to decide," Caius cut in, his voice sharp. "The spell is too complex. It's best left in your hands, Alpha Darkholme."

Damon's eyes flickered, his expression darkening. "You seem very eager to give her up, Caius."

Lyra watched as her brother stiffened, his mask of confidence cracking just slightly. Damon's words carried weight, the threat beneath them subtle but unmistakable.

Damon's sharp gaze turned back to Caius, his patience clearly wearing thin. "You're hiding something, Caius. What aren't you telling me?"

Caius shifted, visibly uncomfortable under Damon's scrutiny. "I've told you everything—her power, her past. You know what's at stake."

Damon crossed his arms, unmoved. "No. You're too desperate for this deal. There's more, and I want to hear it now."

The room fell silent, the weight of Damon's demand hanging in the air. Lyra could see her brother's jaw tighten, his hands clenching into fists. Finally, after a long pause, Caius spoke.

"The spell…" he began, his voice low, "it's not just a simple binding. It's ancient magic. Dark magic. If it's broken wrong, it could unleash her power in ways we can't control."

Lyra's blood ran cold. She hadn't known that. Caius had never told her how dangerous the spell really was. Her wolf was caged, yes, but now it seemed that cage was far more dangerous than she had ever realized.

Damon's expression didn't change, but there was a glint in his eyes, a flicker of interest. "And you did this to your own sister?"

Caius's mask cracked completely this time, his eyes darting to Lyra before quickly looking away. "It was necessary. For her protection—and for the pack's."

Lyra's heart ached at the lie. It had never been about protecting her. It had always been about control.

Damon remained silent, his thoughts unreadable as he processed Caius's words. The tension in the room thickened, the air almost suffocating. Lyra felt like a pawn in a game she didn't understand, her fate being bartered over like she was nothing more than a weapon to be used.

Finally, after what felt like an eternity, Damon spoke.

"I'll take her," he said, his voice steady, but there was a sharpness to it, a promise of something dangerous lurking beneath the surface.

Caius let out a breath he hadn't realized he'd been holding. "Good. I'll have the spell transferred to you immediately."

Lyra's stomach twisted. She had been traded from one cage to another. But Damon turned to her, his eyes meeting hers with an intensity that made her breath catch.

"You want to be free?" he asked again, his voice softer now, almost gentle.

Lyra swallowed, her pulse racing. "Yes."

Damon nodded slowly, then turned back to Caius. "Do it."

As the deal was sealed, Lyra's mind raced. She was no longer under Caius's control, but now she belonged to Damon Darkholme. And she had no idea what that truly meant.

Four

Chapter 4: The Bonded Prisoner.

Lyra stood at the edge of the packhouse, watching as Damon and Caius exchanged clipped words. The sun was just beginning to rise, casting the world in a pale, cold light. Caius had agreed to transfer the binding spell to Damon, but his warning still echoed in Lyra's ears.

"You may think you're free, Lyra," Caius had hissed in her ear moments earlier. "But Damon won't protect you. He's only interested in your power. The moment you lose control, you're as good as dead."

She shivered at the memory, though the chill in the air had little to do with it. Her brother's manipulation dug deep, leaving behind a pit of unease. Could she trust Damon? She had no idea what to expect from him, only that she was walking away from one cage and possibly into another.

Damon approached her, his eyes sharp as he studied her face. "You ready?" His tone was neutral, but there was a weight to his words that suggested much more. Lyra nodded, even though her insides twisted with uncertainty. What choice did she have?

Without another word, he helped her onto his horse, and within minutes, they were riding away from Blackthorn Hollow. Lyra glanced back once, seeing Caius standing at the doorway, his expression unreadable. Her stomach churned, knowing that whatever lay ahead with Damon, she was truly leaving the only life she had known.

As the packhouse disappeared behind them, Damon spoke over his shoulder. "From now on, you answer to me. Don't forget that."

Lyra clenched her jaw and nodded, though her mind raced. His words were clear—she was still under someone's control. But something inside her stirred, faint but undeniable. Maybe, just maybe, this was her first step toward freedom.

The forest around them was thick with fog, the morning light barely piercing through the dense canopy of trees. Damon kept a steady pace, his silence unnerving as they rode deeper into the wilderness. Lyra's thoughts churned in the quiet. She had spent so many years under Caius's thumb, but now, under Damon's control, she wasn't sure if she felt any freer.

"What do you think will happen when your wolf is unbound?" Damon asked suddenly, breaking the silence. His voice was calm, but there was a curiosity there that made Lyra uneasy.

"I don't know," she admitted, her voice soft. The truth was, she didn't even know if she wanted to find out. The memory of losing control that night—her parents lying dead at her feet—still haunted her every day.

Damon glanced back at her, his expression unreadable. "You're stronger than you think," he said after a moment, his tone surprisingly soft. "But if you want to survive, you'll need to control it."

Lyra swallowed hard, unsure if his words were meant to encourage or threaten her. She had felt her wolf stirring recently, more frequently since Damon's arrival, but it was still weak. The thought of unleashing that part of herself both terrified and thrilled her.

Damon's voice cut through her thoughts again. "What Caius didn't tell you is that the binding spell isn't just about control. It's ancient magic, and breaking it wrong could be dangerous."

Lyra's heart skipped a beat. She had always known the spell was powerful, but this was the first time she had heard it could be dangerous to break.

"What happens if it goes wrong?" she asked, her voice barely a whisper.

Damon's gaze flicked toward her, a shadow crossing his face. "You don't want to find out."

Damon led Lyra off the main path, deep into a part of the forest where the trees stood closer together, their twisted branches forming a dark canopy above. She felt a sense of unease creep over her as the light dimmed, shadows lengthening with each step.

"There's something you need to understand," Damon said, stopping near a large oak tree. "Your family's curse—your binding—it's tied to something much older than just pack politics. There's a prophecy."

Lyra blinked, taken aback. "A prophecy?"

Damon nodded, his expression grim. "Your wolf… it's more than just a tool of power. It's part of a bloodline that's been hunted for centuries. Wolves like you are rare, Lyra. You don't just have strength—you have the potential to change everything. For better or for worse."

Lyra felt her breath catch in her throat. Her entire life, she had been told she was dangerous, that her power was a threat. But no one had ever hinted that there was more to it. More to her. "Why didn't Caius tell me?"

"Because Caius is a coward," Damon said bluntly. "He didn't care about you—he cared about what you could do for him. Keeping you bound meant keeping you under his control. But that curse is much older than Caius. And now that the spell is mine to control, there's a lot more at stake."

Lyra felt the ground tilt beneath her feet. Everything she thought she knew about her wolf, about her family, was unraveling before her eyes.

Before Lyra could ask any more questions, the sound of movement cut through the quiet. Damon tensed, his hand flying to the hilt of his sword. The rustling grew louder, and Lyra's heart pounded as several figures emerged from the trees—wolves from Blackthorn Hollow. Leading them was Rourke, Caius's lieutenant, his face twisted into a cruel smile.

"Well, well," Rourke sneered, stepping forward. "Did you really think Caius would let you walk away that easily?"

Damon didn't flinch. "She's no longer yours," he said coldly, stepping in front of Lyra. "And if you value your life, you'll back down."

Rourke laughed, a harsh sound that echoed through the trees. "I'm not afraid of you, Darkholme. Caius gave me strict orders—bring her back, or don't come back at all."

Lyra's wolf stirred violently within her, reacting to the threat, pushing against the edges of the spell that held it captive. Her breath came in short gasps as fear and anger surged inside her. Damon glanced at her, his eyes sharp.

"Stay behind me," he ordered, his voice hard. Then, without another word, he lunged at the nearest wolf.

23

The forest erupted into chaos as Damon clashed with the wolves. Lyra stood frozen, her wolf snarling inside her, desperate to break free. But the spell held firm, trapping her in place as she watched Damon fight.

The fight was brutal, but Damon moved with a lethal grace that left the Blackthorn wolves scrambling. One by one, they fell, blood staining the ground as Damon's blade cut through the air with deadly precision. Lyra watched in awe and horror, the violent clash stirring something deep within her.

As the last wolf collapsed, Damon turned to her, his eyes flashing with barely contained fury. "Control it, Lyra," he warned, his voice tight. "Or you'll lose more than just your wolf."

Her body trembled with the force of her wolf's power, clawing at the edges of the spell. Damon grabbed her shoulders, his grip firm as he forced her to meet his gaze. "Focus. Breathe. Don't let it break free like this."

Lyra squeezed her eyes shut, fighting for control as the wolf raged inside her. Slowly, painfully, she managed to push it back, the energy subsiding just enough for her to catch her breath.

When she opened her eyes, Damon's expression had softened slightly. "This is only the beginning," he said, his voice low. "If you don't learn to master this, others will come. And they'll be a lot worse than Caius's wolves."

Lyra's heart raced as she met his gaze, her voice barely a whisper. "What do you mean? Who's coming?"

Damon's eyes darkened. "Wolves that won't care about freeing you. They'll want to destroy you."

Five

Chapter 5: Secrets in the Shadows

The forest around them was eerily quiet now, the sounds of the earlier battle fading into the distance. Lyra sat on a fallen log, her body still trembling from the intensity of the ambush and the power she had felt rising within her. Damon was nearby, wiping the blood from his sword with slow, methodical movements. His face was hard, his eyes dark with thought as he surveyed the aftermath of the attack.

Lyra couldn't shake the feeling that everything was spiraling out of control. Her wolf had stirred again during the ambush, more violently this time, and the binding spell had barely managed to hold it back. She was losing control, and it terrified her. She glanced at Damon, wondering if he could sense it too—the storm building inside her.

"You're quiet," Damon said, his voice low as he sheathed his sword and approached her.

Lyra swallowed hard. "I don't know how much longer I can hold it in," she admitted, her voice barely above a whisper. She didn't want to admit her fear, but hiding it seemed pointless. Damon already knew.

Damon's gaze was sharp, but not unkind. "You're stronger than you think," he said. "But if you can't control your wolf, you'll be more of a danger to yourself than anyone else."

Lyra's heart raced. She knew he was right. The power she felt growing inside her was unpredictable, and every time it surged, she felt closer to the edge. Damon crouched in front of her, his expression softer now, though still serious.

"We'll get through this," he promised. "But we need to move fast. Others are coming for you. Stronger than Caius. You need to be ready."

"Who?" Lyra asked, her stomach knotting.

Damon's jaw tightened. "Wolves with no loyalty to anyone but themselves. They won't care about you—only what your power can do."

Lyra's blood ran cold. The danger she faced wasn't just about Caius anymore. It was much bigger than that.

Before she could process Damon's words, he froze, his eyes narrowing as he scanned the surrounding trees. "We're being watched," he muttered, drawing his sword again.

From the shadows of the trees, a figure stepped forward—a tall man draped in a dark cloak, his amber eyes gleaming in the dim light. His movements were deliberate, his presence unsettling. Lyra tensed, instinctively moving closer to Damon, though the stranger didn't appear to be hostile.

Damon stepped in front of her, his blade raised defensively. "Who are you?"

he demanded, his voice low but edged with warning.

The man didn't flinch. "I'm not here to fight," he said, his voice calm, almost soothing. He pulled back the hood of his cloak, revealing a weathered face, marked with age and wisdom. "My name is Eamon Graymire."

Damon's eyes narrowed. "What do you want?"

"I've been watching for a long time," Eamon said, his gaze shifting to Lyra. "Watching her."

Lyra's heart skipped a beat, her pulse quickening. She didn't understand how or why this stranger had been following her, but his eyes held a depth of knowledge that made her uneasy.

"What do you know about her?" Damon asked, his voice sharp.

Eamon's eyes never left Lyra. "She is the key. The prophecy foretold her arrival—one with the power to either unite or destroy the wolf clans."

Lyra's mind raced. Prophecies? Power? None of this made sense, but the certainty in Eamon's voice chilled her to the bone. Damon, though wary, seemed to consider the man's words carefully.

"The prophecy," Damon repeated. "You're talking about the curse."

"Yes," Eamon replied. "Her bloodline is tied to an ancient power. She is bound by magic older than any of us. The wolves that hunt her—they know what she's capable of, and they will stop at nothing to control it."

Lyra's stomach turned. She had always been told she was dangerous, but now she understood—this went far beyond Caius's manipulation.

The howls in the distance were growing louder. Damon's eyes hardened as he grabbed Lyra's arm, pulling her into the dense forest without another word. Eamon followed, moving quickly despite his age, keeping pace with them as the distant threat closed in.

"Who's coming?" Lyra asked breathlessly as they ran.

"Hunters," Damon growled. "Wolves who serve no pack. They've heard about you."

Lyra's heart pounded. She hadn't realized how far the danger stretched, and now they were being pursued by more than just Caius's wolves. These hunters, whoever they were, wouldn't stop until they had her.

The forest grew darker as they pushed deeper into the woods, the ground uneven beneath their feet. Damon led the way, navigating the treacherous terrain with ease, but Lyra struggled to keep up, her mind still racing from Eamon's revelation.

"Where are we going?" she called out.

"To a safe place," Damon replied. "We need time to figure out our next move."

The howls were closer now, and Lyra could feel her wolf stirring again, restless and agitated. The sensation was stronger than before, pulsing through her like an electric current. She stumbled, her breath coming in short, panicked gasps.

Damon stopped suddenly, turning to her. "You need to focus, Lyra. If you let your wolf take over now, we're all dead."

Lyra nodded, trying to steady her breathing. But it was hard—her wolf was fighting her, clawing at the edges of the binding spell. Damon's grip tightened on her arm, and for a moment, their eyes locked.

"We can't afford a mistake," he said, his voice low but intense.

Before Lyra could respond, the wolves burst through the trees, surrounding them in a deadly semicircle. Damon drew his sword, his stance protective, ready to fight. Eamon stepped back, watching closely but offering no help.

Lyra's heart raced. The wolves were snarling, their eyes fixed on her as if they could sense the power building inside her. Fear gripped her, but something else surged with it—anger.

Her wolf pushed harder now, the binding spell cracking under the force of it. She felt it rising, clawing its way to the surface, desperate to break free. Damon glanced at her, sensing the shift.

"Control it, Lyra," he warned, his voice tight with urgency. "Don't let it break through."

But she couldn't stop it. The power was too much, too fierce. With a shattering force, the binding spell finally gave way, and her wolf exploded from within her, sending a shockwave through the air that knocked the wolves back.

Damon staggered but stayed on his feet, his eyes wide as he took in the sight of her. Lyra stood tall, her body thrumming with energy, her eyes glowing with the power of her wolf. It was overwhelming, terrifying—and exhilarating.

The wolves hesitated, momentarily stunned by the sheer force of Lyra's power. Damon's gaze never left her, but there was no fear in his eyes—only a deep, unspoken understanding of what she had just become.

Lyra's world blurred as the power surged through her, wild and uncontrollable. She could feel her wolf taking over, its hunger for freedom overpowering her will. She tried to pull back, to regain control, but it was like trying to stop a raging storm with bare hands.

Damon stepped forward, his face calm but his eyes burning with intensity. "You have to control it, Lyra," he said, his voice cutting through the chaos in her mind. "If you don't, this power will consume you."

His words broke through the fog, and Lyra focused on his voice, using it as an anchor. She breathed deeply, fighting to push her wolf back, to rein in the overwhelming energy that threatened to swallow her whole. Slowly, agonizingly, she regained control, though the effort left her trembling and weak.

Damon watched her closely, his hand resting lightly on her shoulder. "You did it," he said quietly, though his expression was still serious. "But this is just the beginning."

Lyra nodded, though her body felt like it had been torn apart and put back together again. She knew he was right. The binding spell was fractured, and though she had managed to pull her wolf back this time, there was no guarantee she could do it again.

Eamon stepped forward, his eyes gleaming with a knowing look. "You have great power, Lyra," he said, his voice soft but filled with meaning. "But power like this comes with a price."

Lyra's heart pounded as she met Damon's gaze. She knew what Eamon was saying was true. She had tasted the power of her wolf, and now, nothing would ever be the same.

Six

Chapter 6: A Fateful Revelation

Lyra's legs wobbled as she leaned against a tree, still trembling from the battle. She barely had the strength to hold herself up, and her chest heaved with exhaustion. Damon stood beside her, his expression unreadable, his hand resting on the hilt of his sword as though expecting another attack at any moment. The ambush had pushed Lyra to the edge, but it was the surge of her wolf's power that frightened her the most. She had come so close to losing control.

"You did well," Damon said quietly, his voice calm but edged with something harder.

Lyra wiped the sweat from her brow, her mind still spinning. "Did I?" she asked, her voice shaking. "I almost lost it… again. I don't know how much longer I can keep holding back."

Damon's gaze flickered toward her, but he didn't reply immediately. Instead, he crouched down to tend to a small wound on his arm, speaking as he worked. "You're still here, aren't you? That's what matters. Control is a struggle, but it's one you've already proven you can win."

Lyra wanted to believe him, but doubt gnawed at her. The power she had felt rising inside her during the battle wasn't something she could simply bury. It was wild, untamable, and every time she tried to push it down, it only grew stronger.

Eamon stood a few feet away, watching them both with unsettling calm. "We're running out of time," he said, his voice carrying a weight that cut through the tension. "The lunar eclipse approaches, and with it, the prophecy."

Damon stiffened, turning to face him. "What do you mean?"

"The prophecy doesn't just speak of Lyra's power," Eamon continued, his eyes darkening. "It speaks of a trial. The eclipse will either break the curse binding her wolf, or it will consume her entirely."

Lyra's heart pounded in her chest. The word "consume" echoed in her mind, a terrifying possibility she hadn't considered. She looked at Damon, fear flashing in her eyes, but before she could speak, Eamon stepped forward.

"There is a place where the curse can be broken," he said. "But it's dangerous, and if we don't get there before the eclipse, Lyra may not survive."

As they moved deeper into the forest, Lyra's mind churned with Eamon's words. She was still reeling from the idea of a trial—something tied to the lunar eclipse that would decide her fate. For years, she had believed that the binding spell on her wolf was her greatest problem, but now she realized that breaking it might lead to something far worse.

"What exactly is this trial?" Lyra asked, her voice barely above a whisper. She didn't like the tension that had settled over them, the way Eamon's words carried an unspoken sense of dread.

Eamon walked ahead, his cloak blending into the shadows as he spoke without looking back. "The prophecy speaks of an ancient magic tied to your bloodline, Lyra. It's not just about your wolf. It's about the power within you, something far older than you realize. When the eclipse comes, that magic will rise. If you cannot control it, it will destroy you."

Lyra felt a chill run down her spine. Destroy her? The thought of facing a power she couldn't control, a power that might consume her completely, made her stomach twist in fear.

Damon slowed his pace, falling in step beside her. His face was tense, his eyes hard as he processed what Eamon had said. "You're stronger than this," he told her, his voice quiet but firm. "We'll figure this out."

But Eamon's warnings hung in the air like a storm cloud. "Even if she's strong," Eamon said, "strength alone won't be enough. The temple where the curse can be broken is hidden in the mountains, guarded by ancient forces that will not let us pass easily."

Lyra's heart raced. A trial, a temple, ancient forces—all of it felt like something out of a nightmare. She wasn't ready for this. How could she be?

The three of them continued through the forest, the trees closing in around them as they followed a narrow path that wound deeper into the wilderness. The air grew colder, and the distant sounds of animals faded until all that remained was the rustle of leaves beneath their feet.

Damon was quiet, his thoughts clearly focused on what lay ahead. Eamon led the way, his movements smooth and unhurried despite the urgency of their mission. Lyra's mind, however, was racing.

"What happens if I can't control it?" Lyra asked, breaking the silence. The question had been gnawing at her since Eamon had mentioned the eclipse.

33

Eamon didn't answer right away. He paused, glancing over his shoulder at her before speaking. "If you lose control during the trial, the power within you will be unleashed without restraint. It will consume everything in its path—your wolf, your humanity, everything."

Lyra's chest tightened. The thought of losing herself, of becoming something she couldn't recognize, terrified her. She had spent so long fearing the power of her wolf, but now it seemed like the wolf was only a part of a much larger problem.

Damon's voice cut through the tension. "We'll make it to the temple before the eclipse. You'll get through this, Lyra."

But Lyra wasn't so sure. "What if we don't?" she asked, her voice trembling despite her efforts to keep it steady.

Damon's gaze softened, but there was steel behind his words. "Then we'll face whatever comes. Together."

Eamon stopped suddenly, raising a hand to signal silence. His sharp gaze scanned the forest, and Damon's hand instinctively moved to his sword. The air felt heavier now, thick with the sense of something lurking nearby.

"We're not alone," Damon muttered, his voice low.

Before they could move, shadows shifted around them, and a low growl rumbled through the air. Damon unsheathed his sword in a fluid motion, his body tensing as several wolves emerged from the trees. Leading them was a tall, broad-shouldered Alpha with a menacing grin—Vorn, his eyes gleaming with malice.

"Well, well," Vorn said, his voice a cruel drawl. "Looks like I found what I was looking for."

Lyra's blood ran cold as Vorn's gaze settled on her. She could feel the hunger in his eyes, the way he looked at her like she was a prize to be claimed. Damon stepped forward, placing himself between her and Vorn.

"You're not taking her," Damon growled, his voice a low warning.

Vorn's grin widened. "You can't stop me, Darkholme. She belongs with me now."

The tension snapped like a wire pulled too tight. In an instant, Vorn's wolves attacked, their fangs bared and their growls filling the air. Damon met them head-on, his sword flashing as he cut through the first wave of attackers. Eamon moved with deadly precision, his speed surprising for someone of his age.

But Lyra's focus was on Vorn. He taunted her from the sidelines, his voice cutting through the chaos. "You think you can control that power inside you? You're a fool. Let it out, Lyra. Embrace what you are."

Her wolf stirred violently at his words, pushing against the remnants of the binding spell. The temptation to let go, to unleash the full force of her wolf, was overwhelming.

Lyra's body trembled as her wolf surged within her, its power too strong to contain. Vorn's words echoed in her mind, feeding her fears. "You're not ready," he sneered. "You'll never be ready."

Her vision blurred as the power rose, threatening to break free. She felt herself slipping, losing control, the binding spell cracking under the pressure. Just as she was about to give in, Damon's voice cut through the fog of her thoughts.

"Lyra!" he shouted, his voice sharp with urgency. "Don't let him win. You're

35

stronger than this."

His words pierced the haze, grounding her for a moment. Lyra gasped, struggling to regain control, but the power was relentless, surging through her like a storm. Damon reached her, his hand gripping her arm, his eyes locking onto hers.

"Focus on me," he commanded, his voice steady despite the chaos around them. "You can do this."

Lyra closed her eyes, forcing herself to breathe, to push back the power threatening to overwhelm her. Slowly, painfully, she regained control, her wolf retreating into the depths of her mind. But the effort left her shaking, her body weak.

Vorn's wolves retreated, but the damage had been done. Lyra knew that the next time she might not be able to hold back.

Eamon watched from a distance, his expression unreadable. The trial at the temple loomed closer, and Lyra knew that if she couldn't control her power then, it would consume her completely.

"We're running out of time," Damon said quietly, his voice grim. "The eclipse is coming."

Lyra looked up at the sky, the moon barely visible through the trees. The eclipse was fast approaching, and with it, the trial that would determine her fate.

Seven

Chapter 7: The Journey to the Temple

The wind howled as they began their ascent, the mountain looming above them like a silent sentinel. The path was narrow, winding between jagged rocks and patches of ice that glistened under the pale light of the moon. Lyra struggled to keep up, her legs burning from the strain of the climb, her body still recovering from the battle with Vorn's wolves. Every step felt heavier than the last, but she forced herself to keep moving.

Damon glanced back at her, his expression tense. "You holding up?" he asked, his voice cutting through the cold air.

Lyra nodded, though she wasn't sure how much longer she could hold on. The weight of the prophecy hung over her, pressing down with every step she took. She wasn't just climbing a mountain; she was climbing toward a fate she didn't fully understand.

Eamon, leading the way, moved with an eerie calm. His footsteps were sure and steady, as if the treacherous terrain didn't bother him at all. Lyra watched him, uneasy. There was something about the way he navigated the path that unsettled her, like he knew something they didn't.

"The closer we get to the temple, the stronger the magic becomes," Eamon said, his voice carrying easily over the wind. "It will test us—try to turn us back. You must stay focused."

Lyra swallowed hard. The idea of facing more magic, especially after the illusions in the forest, made her stomach twist. But there was no other choice. The temple was her only chance to break the curse.

The path grew steeper, and as they climbed higher, Lyra felt the air thinning. Her chest tightened, each breath a struggle, but she kept moving, her gaze fixed on Damon's back. She didn't know what the temple would ask of her, but she knew one thing for sure—whatever lay ahead, she couldn't face it alone.

The first sign that something was wrong came in the form of a subtle shift in the air. Lyra blinked, feeling dizzy for a moment. When she looked around, the trees seemed to have moved, their branches twisting unnaturally. The path that had been clear just seconds before now stretched endlessly into the distance, the landscape warping before her eyes.

Damon noticed it too. "Stay close," he ordered, gripping his sword tightly.

Eamon's voice was calm but firm. "The illusions have begun. Don't trust what you see."

Lyra's heart raced as the trees around her twisted and shifted, their gnarled branches reaching out like claws. The path beneath her feet seemed to disappear, leaving her standing on nothing but empty air. She stumbled, panic rising in her chest, but Damon caught her arm, pulling her back to solid ground.

"Focus," he said, his voice steady. "None of this is real."

But it felt real. The wind, the cold, the weight of the illusions pressed down on her, distorting her sense of reality. And then, in the corner of her vision, she saw something—someone. A figure standing just beyond the trees, cloaked in shadow.

"Mom?" Lyra whispered, her voice barely audible.

The figure didn't move, but Lyra's heart ached at the sight. It was her mother, or at least, it looked like her. But Lyra knew it couldn't be real. Her mother had been gone for years.

"Lyra, don't look at it!" Damon's voice snapped her back to reality, but the vision didn't disappear.

Tears welled in her eyes as she tore her gaze away, forcing herself to focus on the path. The illusions were playing tricks on her, showing her what she wanted most. It was cruel, and it took every ounce of willpower to keep moving.

The illusions faded as they climbed higher, but the sense of unease lingered. The air grew colder, sharper, and the wind howled through the rocky crags. Then, without warning, a deep growl echoed through the mountain pass, sending a shiver down Lyra's spine.

Damon drew his sword, his eyes scanning the darkness. "Stay behind me," he said, his voice low.

From the shadows emerged a massive wolf, its body shimmering with an otherworldly light. Its eyes glowed, burning with an intensity that made

Lyra's blood run cold. Eamon stepped forward, his expression unreadable.

"The guardian," he said quietly. "It's here to test you."

The wolf growled again, its gaze locking onto Lyra. She felt the power of her wolf stirring within her, reacting to the presence of the guardian. The creature wasn't just any wolf—it was a manifestation of the temple's magic, a guardian set to challenge those who sought to enter.

"You must face it," Eamon said, his voice calm. "This is your trial, Lyra."

Damon moved to protest, but Eamon shook his head. "She must do this alone."

Lyra's heart pounded in her chest as she stepped forward, her hands trembling. The wolf's growl deepened, its eyes glowing brighter. She could feel the pull of her wolf, the power rising within her, but she was afraid—afraid of what might happen if she lost control.

The guardian wolf lunged, its massive form barreling toward her. Lyra stood her ground, her eyes glowing as she called upon her wolf, but the power was wild, untamed, and she struggled to rein it in.

Lyra's heart thundered in her chest as the guardian wolf circled her, its glowing eyes never leaving hers. She could feel the power of her wolf surging within her, raw and dangerous, but she had no choice. This was her trial—she had to face it alone.

The air crackled with energy as Lyra closed her eyes, reaching deep inside herself to find control. Her wolf was there, waiting, but it was wild, resisting her touch. She took a deep breath, forcing herself to calm her racing thoughts.

"Focus," she whispered to herself. "I can do this."

The guardian wolf growled, its breath hot against her skin as it stalked closer. Lyra opened her eyes, her gaze locking with the creature's. For a moment, everything else faded—the wind, the cold, the fear. All that remained was the power thrumming inside her, waiting to be unleashed.

Lyra's hands glowed faintly as she called on her wolf, the energy swirling around her. She could feel the binding spell cracking, the magic that had held her wolf at bay for so long beginning to unravel. But this time, she didn't fight it.

The power surged through her, filling every inch of her body with heat and strength. The guardian wolf growled again, but this time, Lyra didn't flinch. She met its gaze with a fierce determination, her own wolf rising to the surface.

The ground trembled beneath her feet as the energy reached its peak. Lyra took a step forward, her hands glowing brighter as she released the power in a controlled burst. The guardian wolf howled, its spectral form flickering for a moment before it disappeared into the mist.

Lyra stood there, breathing heavily, her body shaking from the effort. She had done it. She had controlled her wolf, if only for a moment.

The victory was short-lived. As soon as the guardian disappeared, the ground beneath them began to shake violently. Rocks tumbled down the mountainside, and the path ahead cracked and splintered, threatening to collapse.

"Move!" Damon shouted, grabbing Lyra's arm and pulling her forward.

The air was filled with the sound of crumbling stone as the ground gave way beneath their feet. Lyra's heart raced as she stumbled, her legs heavy with exhaustion. Damon's grip on her tightened as they leaped over a widening chasm, the earth breaking apart behind them.

Eamon was already ahead, his movements quick and precise as he navigated the collapsing path. "We're almost there!" he called out, his voice barely audible over the roar of the mountain.

Lyra's breath came in ragged gasps as they raced toward the entrance of the temple, the ground crumbling beneath them. Just as they reached the final stretch of the path, a massive section of the cliff gave way, leaving a gaping hole between them and the temple.

Damon leaped across with ease, but Lyra stumbled, her foot slipping on the loose rocks. She teetered on the edge, her heart hammering in her chest as she struggled to regain her balance. Just as she was about to fall, Damon's hand shot out, grabbing hers and pulling her to safety.

They collapsed onto the solid ground in front of the temple, breathing heavily. Lyra's body shook with exhaustion, but she was alive. She looked up at the towering stone doors, her heart still racing.

Eamon stood at the entrance, his expression unreadable. "This was only the beginning," he said quietly. "The real trial is yet to come."

The massive stone doors of the temple creaked open, revealing only darkness beyond.

Eight

Chapter 8: The Trials Within the Temple

The heavy stone doors slammed shut behind them with a resounding finality, casting the chamber into near-total darkness. The oppressive silence of the temple enveloped Lyra, Damon, and Eamon, sending a chill through the air. Lyra's breath came out in short, nervous gasps, her heartbeat pounding in her ears as they stepped deeper into the cavernous hall. Only the faint, eerie glow of the ancient runes on the walls offered any light, their dim pulse in sync with the thrum of magic that filled the air.

"This place is alive," Lyra murmured, her voice barely above a whisper.

Eamon nodded gravely. "The temple's magic is sentient, designed to challenge and break intruders. It will force you to face the truth of who you are—and what you fear."

Damon remained silent, his hand resting on the hilt of his sword. His eyes darted around, alert for any danger. His presence beside Lyra was a comfort, but the weight of what she faced pressed down on her. This temple wasn't just a physical trial—it was a test of her will, her strength, and her control over the wolf raging inside her.

As they ventured further into the temple, Lyra felt a strange pull deep within her chest. It was as if the very walls were alive, resonating with the power that had been bound within her for so long. The prophecy was real. This was the place where she would either break the curse or be consumed by it.

The path narrowed, leading them into a deeper chamber. Lyra's pulse quickened, every step making the air heavier. Suddenly, the ground beneath them shifted, and before anyone could react, Damon was yanked into the shadows by an unseen force.

"Damon!" Lyra cried, her voice echoing through the chamber as the darkness swallowed him whole.

Lyra's heart pounded as Damon vanished into the blackness. The temple seemed to swallow him without a trace, leaving her alone with Eamon. The oppressive silence that followed his disappearance was suffocating, and panic welled up inside her.

"Where did he go?" Lyra demanded, her voice cracking with fear.

Eamon remained calm, his expression unreadable. "This is the temple's way. It isolates each of us, forcing us to face our trials alone. Damon will have his own battle, as will you. The temple tests our will—our ability to conquer what lies within."

"But I need him!" Lyra's voice wavered. "I can't—"

"You can," Eamon interrupted, his tone firm. "This is your trial, Lyra. You must face it without relying on him."

Lyra swallowed hard, the weight of Eamon's words sinking in. She hated the idea of being separated from Damon, but there was no choice. The temple would challenge her in ways she couldn't predict, and she would have to face it alone.

As they pressed deeper into the temple, the air grew colder, and the shadows seemed to stretch toward her, twisting and shifting like living entities. Faint whispers began to echo through the chamber, voices she recognized all too well. They were memories—twisted fragments of the night her parents died, of Caius's betrayal, of everything that haunted her.

The voices grew louder, accusing her, taunting her for her failures. Her hands clenched into fists as the wolf inside her stirred, restless and angry. She could feel it clawing at the edges of the binding spell, desperate to break free.

"Focus," Eamon said quietly. "The temple is testing you. It knows your fears."

But it wasn't just fear. It was guilt. Guilt for what she'd done, for the blood on her hands, and for the wolf she couldn't control.

The shadows twisted around Lyra, forming into familiar shapes. The cold, accusing eyes of her brother Caius stared at her from the darkness, his voice a venomous whisper.

"You were always weak, Lyra. You couldn't even protect them."

She flinched, the weight of his words like a blow to the chest. The figure of Caius circled her, his expression twisted with disdain. Her heart raced as the memories she had fought to bury surged to the surface. She could still see the bodies of her parents, lifeless on the ground, the blood on her hands, the power she had unleashed in a moment of uncontrollable rage.

"No," Lyra whispered, shaking her head. "It wasn't my fault."

But the temple seemed to feed on her guilt, amplifying her doubts. Another figure emerged from the shadows—her mother, her face filled with sorrow. Lyra's breath hitched as the illusion whispered, "You could have saved us."

The wolf inside her roared, pushing harder against the binding spell, desperate to break free and silence the voices. Her hands began to glow faintly with magic, the power building, wild and untamed.

"You have to control it," Eamon's voice broke through the chaos, distant but steady. "If you lose yourself now, the temple wins."

Lyra closed her eyes, trying to block out the illusions. She took a deep breath, focusing on the words Damon had spoken to her before—*You're stronger than this*. Slowly, she reached for the power within her, but this time, instead of fighting it, she accepted it.

The energy surged through her, filling her with strength, but she didn't let it overwhelm her. She took control, forcing the wolf to submit. The shadows around her began to fade, the whispers dying away as the temple acknowledged her resolve.

But she knew this was only the beginning.

As the illusions faded, a low, menacing growl echoed through the chamber. Lyra's heart skipped a beat as the ground trembled beneath her feet. Out of the shadows emerged the spectral wolf guardian, its massive form even more imposing than before. Its eyes glowed with the same strange magic that pulsed through the temple, watching her with a predatory intensity.

"This is your next trial," Eamon said quietly. "The temple will test your strength—both physical and magical."

The guardian wolf circled Lyra, its growl reverberating through the stone chamber. She felt her wolf stir in response, the power rising again within her. This time, she didn't try to suppress it. She knew the temple wouldn't let her pass unless she proved she could harness the strength of her wolf.

The guardian lunged at her, moving with impossible speed. Lyra barely had time to react, diving to the side as its massive claws slashed through the air where she had been standing. She rolled to her feet, her hands glowing with the energy of her wolf as she faced the creature head-on.

The battle was fierce, the guardian attacking relentlessly while Lyra fought to keep up. Her wolf gave her strength and speed, but every time she called on its power, she felt the binding spell weaken further. She couldn't afford to lose control now—not when the temple was still testing her.

The guardian lunged again, its claws aiming for her throat. Lyra ducked beneath the attack, her body moving with a grace she hadn't felt in years. She summoned a burst of energy, her hands glowing brighter as she struck back, sending the guardian skidding across the stone floor.

The creature growled, but it didn't attack again. Instead, it vanished into the shadows, leaving Lyra standing in the center of the chamber, breathless and trembling.

Lyra barely had time to catch her breath before the walls of the temple shifted once more. The ground beneath her feet seemed to ripple, the ancient stone groaning as a new doorway appeared at the far end of the chamber. Eamon stepped forward, his expression as unreadable as ever.

"This is it," he said. "The heart of the temple."

Lyra's heart pounded as she followed him into the final chamber. The room was massive, its ceiling stretching high above them, lined with ancient runes that pulsed with a soft, glowing light. In the center of the room was a stone altar, and on it lay a crystal, glowing with the same strange magic that filled the temple.

"This crystal holds the power to break the curse," Eamon explained. "But it will require all of your strength, all of your control. If you cannot master your wolf now, the temple will consume you."

Lyra's pulse quickened as she stepped toward the altar. The power radiating from the crystal was overwhelming, calling to the magic within her. Her wolf surged in response, the binding spell snapping under the pressure. She could feel the full force of her wolf rising within her, wild and uncontrollable.

Damon's voice echoed in her mind, though she still couldn't see him. "Lyra, be careful. Don't trust it."

But Lyra knew this was the moment she had been preparing for. She reached out, her fingers trembling as they closed around the crystal. The magic surged through her, and for a brief moment, she felt herself slipping away into the power.

The room was flooded with light as the power overtook her, and Lyra's vision blurred. Somewhere in the distance, she heard Damon's voice again, but it was drowned out by the roar of her wolf.

Here is Chapter 9: The Heart of the Prophecy, written across five scenes with each scene at 600 words to reach the 3,000-word count goal. Each scene builds tension and action, progressing naturally toward the climax and ending with a meaningful cliffhanger.

Nine

Chapter 9: The Heart of the Prophecy

The crystal pulsed in Lyra's hand, its light blinding as it filled the chamber. The raw power it held surged through her body, crackling like lightning under her skin. Lyra gasped, her mind reeling as the magic overwhelmed her. It was too much. She could feel her wolf, wild and untamed, rising to the surface, the barriers that had kept it at bay now shattered.

The binding spell that had restrained her wolf for so long snapped, its hold on her broken completely. A rush of energy exploded within her, and for a moment, she lost all sense of herself. The line between her and the beast blurred, and the wolf's hunger, its primal need to run free, roared inside her mind.

"Lyra!" Damon's voice echoed distantly, but it felt miles away. She was drowning in the power, her vision flickering between flashes of the temple and an endless void of pure energy.

The whispers grew louder, tugging at her consciousness. They urged her to surrender, to let the wolf take over, to forget the burden of control. It would be so easy to give in. The strength, the freedom—it was all right there, waiting for her. But beneath that promise, there was something darker. A voice warning her of what would happen if she lost herself entirely.

Lyra gritted her teeth, fighting to hold on. She couldn't let the wolf consume her, not now. She focused on the sound of Damon's voice, anchoring herself to the one thing that had kept her grounded through all of this.

As the power raged within her, she heard something else—a low growl that vibrated through her chest. She blinked, and suddenly, she wasn't in the temple anymore. She stood in the middle of a forest, the moon casting long shadows across the trees.

Lyra looked around, her breath coming in shallow gasps. The temple was gone, replaced by the familiar scent of pine and earth. Her body had shifted without her realizing it—she was in her wolf form, her paws pressing into the damp soil beneath her. Every sense was heightened: the crisp air, the rustling of leaves, the distant call of another wolf. But something felt wrong. This wasn't real.

She was caught in another vision.

"Lyra," Damon's voice called from somewhere in the distance, urgent but echoing as if from far away. She looked around, her heart racing, trying to find him. But the more she searched, the thicker the trees seemed to grow, closing in around her like a cage.

She ran, her powerful legs carrying her deeper into the forest, following the sound of Damon's voice. The energy from the crystal still pulsed inside her, but here, in this strange dream, it was more controlled. She could feel her wolf, but it wasn't wild anymore. It was as if the vision had placed a temporary calm over the chaos inside her.

As she moved through the forest, shadows shifted in the trees. Images from her past—ghostly figures of her parents, of Caius—flickered at the edges of her vision. Her breath caught in her throat as the memories resurfaced. The night her parents had died, the fear in their eyes as the power inside her had unleashed. The guilt she'd carried for so long threatened to pull her under again.

But there was no time to dwell. She needed to find Damon, needed to get out of this illusion before it consumed her.

"Lyra…" The voice came again, closer this time. She pushed through the underbrush, her heart pounding as she broke into a clearing. But instead of Damon, she came face-to-face with a figure she hadn't expected.

Caius.

Caius stood before her, his form as solid as if he were truly there. His eyes gleamed with a familiar malice, his lips twisting into a cruel smile. Lyra's heart froze. This was the last thing she wanted to see—the brother who had betrayed her, the one who had twisted her fate and kept her bound in chains.

"You'll never control it," Caius sneered, stepping closer. "You think you've grown stronger, but you're the same weak girl you always were. You'll lose control, just like before. And when you do, you'll destroy everything."

Lyra's wolf stirred violently, reacting to the threat, the anger. Her claws dug into the earth, her breath coming out in low, steady growls. The magic inside her burned hot, and she could feel the pull of the power again, urging her to fight, to let go.

But Caius's words struck at her deepest fear. She remembered the night their parents had died, how she had lost control and the wolf had torn through everything. The guilt hit her like a tidal wave, and for a moment, she faltered.

"You don't belong here," she growled, but the doubt in her voice was clear.

Caius's laugh was cold and hollow. "You'll never escape what you are."

The pressure built inside her, the power rising again. It was like standing on the edge of a cliff, teetering between falling and flying. But as the rage threatened to pull her under, Damon's voice cut through the haze.

"Lyra! Don't listen to him. You're stronger than this."

Lyra blinked, the sound of Damon's voice steadying her. The wolf inside her raged, but this time she didn't let it take over. She focused, drawing on every ounce of control she had fought so hard to build.

"I won't let you control me anymore," she said, her voice firm now.

With a surge of power, she lashed out, shattering the illusion of Caius. His form dissolved into nothing, and the clearing around her blurred.

The vision of the forest faded, and Lyra found herself standing once again in the heart of the temple. The crystal still pulsed in her hand, its light illuminating the chamber with an eerie glow. She was breathless, her mind reeling from the confrontation with Caius's illusion. But something had shifted inside her. The guilt that had once weighed her down no longer had the same hold.

"You've passed the test," Eamon's voice echoed softly from behind her. He stood at the edge of the chamber, his face unreadable. "But now, the choice is yours."

Lyra's hands trembled as she looked down at the glowing crystal. The power inside it thrummed, echoing the energy that still surged through her veins. She knew what came next—if she wanted to break the curse, she would have to unleash the full power of her wolf. But the thought of doing so filled her with both anticipation and dread.

"If you let it out," Eamon continued, his tone grave, "you will face the full force of your power. But if you lose control now, the prophecy will consume you."

Damon's voice came again, this time clearer. "Lyra, you can do this. I believe in you."

His words sent a wave of calm through her, but the fear still lingered. What if she wasn't ready? What if the wolf was too strong?

Lyra took a deep breath, steadying herself. She had come this far. She had faced the illusions, fought her past, and survived the trials of the temple. Now, the final choice lay in her hands.

Her eyes glowed faintly as she tightened her grip on the crystal. The room trembled around her, the magic responding to her will.

The temple shook as the magic inside the crystal surged, flooding the chamber with light. Lyra's heart raced, her pulse in sync with the raw power that flowed through her. The wolf inside her howled, no longer bound by the spell that had kept it contained for so long. The air around her crackled with energy, the force of it nearly overwhelming.

Eamon stood back, watching as the power built. "The prophecy has led you here," he said quietly. "Now, it's time for you to fulfill it."

Lyra closed her eyes, feeling the full weight of the decision before her. She could sense the power waiting, ready to be unleashed. But this time, she wasn't afraid. She knew what she had to do.

With a deep breath, Lyra raised the crystal above her head, the energy pulsing brighter with each passing second. The ground beneath her feet trembled, and the walls of the temple groaned under the pressure of the magic.

Damon's voice echoed in her mind, steady and reassuring. "You're stronger than you think. You've always been."

Lyra's eyes snapped open, glowing with the intensity of her wolf's power. She let out a sharp breath and released the energy, allowing the full force of her wolf to flood the chamber. The crystal shattered in her hands, and the light exploded outward, shaking the temple to its very foundation.

The air was filled with a deafening roar as the magic tore through the room. Lyra felt the power consume her, but this time, she didn't resist. She embraced it, letting the wolf's strength flow through her without fear.

As the light began to fade, Lyra collapsed to the floor, her body drained from the release. The temple was silent, but something felt incomplete. The curse was not yet broken.

Eamon's voice was quiet but foreboding. "It's not over."

Ten

Chapter 10: The Final Trial

Lyra lay on the cold stone floor, her breath ragged, her body trembling from the overwhelming surge of power she had just unleashed. The crystal had shattered in her hands, the once blinding light fading into a dim glow that left the temple eerily silent. For a moment, she thought it was over. She had released the wolf, taken control, and yet... something was wrong.

The curse hadn't broken.

She struggled to rise, her legs shaking beneath her. Her wolf was still with her—strong, fierce—but the oppressive weight of the curse hadn't lifted. The air around her seemed heavier, and a deep cold had settled into the chamber, as if the temple itself was waiting for something.

Damon's voice, faint but steady, echoed in her mind. "Lyra... are you okay?"

She tried to respond, but her throat was dry, the words stuck behind the exhaustion that threatened to pull her under. She had fought so hard to control the wolf, to accept it as part of her, and yet she still wasn't free.

Eamon's shadow fell over her, his expression unreadable. "You're not done," he said quietly, his voice carrying a weight that made Lyra's heart tighten. "There is one final trial—the curse itself."

Lyra's eyes widened as she forced herself to stand. "The curse... it's still here?"

Eamon nodded. "The power you unleashed was necessary, but the curse has always been more than just magic. It is bound to your soul, to the fear and guilt you've carried. You'll have to face it, or it will consume your wolf... and you."

The realization hit her like a wave of ice. The curse was still alive, and it wasn't done with her yet.

A low, chilling wind swept through the temple, carrying with it a darkness that seemed to swallow the faint light of the glowing runes on the walls. Lyra's breath hitched as the temperature in the chamber dropped, the air growing thick with tension. Slowly, a shadow began to take form in the center of the room, swirling and coiling like smoke before solidifying into something more menacing.

The curse.

It took shape before her—a towering, formless figure made of shadows, its presence suffocating. The darkness flickered and shifted, never quite settling into a clear form, but its eyes... its eyes were piercing. Cold and empty, they locked onto Lyra with an intensity that made her blood run cold.

"You think you've won?" the curse hissed, its voice like nails on glass, scraping through her mind. "You think unleashing the wolf will set you free? You are bound to me, Lyra. You always have been."

Lyra's heart pounded in her chest. The curse's voice was like a storm inside her head, whispering of every fear, every doubt she had ever carried. Her hands trembled as the weight of it pressed down on her.

"I've embraced the wolf," she said, her voice shaking but determined. "You don't control me anymore."

The curse laughed, a dark, hollow sound that echoed through the temple. "The wolf is mine. It always has been. And now, you'll watch as it destroys everything."

Lyra's wolf stirred within her, reacting to the threat. She could feel its power rising, but the curse's influence was strong, tightening around her like invisible chains.

Lyra felt the chains of the curse tightening around her, squeezing the air from her lungs. Her wolf, once so close, so familiar, now felt distant. She could feel the power slipping away from her, the connection weakening with every breath. Panic clawed at her chest, threatening to pull her under.

The curse fed on her fear, its laughter growing louder, sharper. "You'll never be free of me, Lyra. You're too weak."

For a moment, Lyra believed it. The memories of the past, the lives she had hurt, the destruction she had caused—they all flooded back with brutal clarity. Her parents' terrified faces, Caius's betrayal, the blood on her hands. The weight of it all crushed her, and she fell to her knees, unable to fight back.

But then, through the darkness, Damon's voice broke through again, stronger this time. "Lyra! Don't give in to it. You're stronger than this. You've already proven that."

His voice was an anchor, pulling her back from the edge of despair. Lyra closed her eyes, forcing herself to breathe. She focused on Damon's words, on the journey she had taken to get here. She had faced the wolf, had accepted it as part of her. She had fought through the trials of the temple, survived the illusions, the fear, the guilt. She wasn't the same person who had walked into this cursed place.

The curse might have power over her past, but it didn't control her future.

With a deep breath, Lyra pushed back against the curse's influence. Slowly, she stood, her legs shaking but steady. Her eyes glowed faintly as the connection to her wolf grew stronger, the chains of the curse loosening.

The curse recoiled as Lyra regained her strength, its shadowy form flickering with anger. The chains that had bound her wolf began to weaken, cracks forming in the darkness that surrounded her. Lyra could feel the power building inside her again, her wolf responding to the threat with a low, deep growl that echoed in her mind.

"You think you can defeat me?" the curse spat, its voice rising with fury. "I am bound to you. I am your fear, your guilt. You cannot escape me."

Lyra stepped forward, her eyes glowing brighter with the energy of her wolf. She had feared this moment for so long, had been terrified of the power she held inside her. But not anymore.

"I'm not afraid of you," she said, her voice calm, steady. "I've faced my past, and I've accepted my wolf. You don't control me anymore."

The curse let out a screech, its shadowy form swelling as it lashed out at her, waves of darkness crashing toward her like a storm. But Lyra didn't flinch. She raised her hands, summoning the power of her wolf, the magic flowing through her like fire. The air crackled with energy as the two forces collided, light and dark battling for dominance.

Lyra pushed harder, her strength growing with every second. She could feel the curse weakening, its grip on her soul slipping. The chains that had bound her wolf for so long shattered, and for the first time, Lyra felt truly free.

But the curse wasn't finished yet.

The final blow came in a blinding surge of light. Lyra gathered all her strength, every ounce of power she had fought so hard to control, and released it in one final, devastating attack. The curse screamed, its shadowy form writhing and twisting as the light consumed it, tearing it apart piece by piece.

For a moment, the temple was filled with a deafening roar, the magic shaking the very foundations of the ancient structure. Lyra stood in the center of it all, her body glowing with the power of her wolf, her heart racing as she channeled the last of her energy into breaking the curse.

The darkness receded, the shadowy figure dissolving into nothing. The curse let out one final, agonized wail before it disappeared completely, leaving only silence in its wake.

Lyra fell to her knees, the weight of the battle catching up with her. Her body ached, her energy spent, but she had done it. The curse was broken.

Eamon stepped forward, his expression one of quiet awe. "It's over," he said softly. "You've won."

Lyra could hardly believe it. The curse that had haunted her for so long, that had bound her wolf and controlled her life, was finally gone. She was free.

But before she could fully take in the victory, Damon appeared beside her, his arms wrapping around her in a tight embrace. "You did it," he whispered, his voice filled with pride. "It's over."

Lyra leaned into him, her heart still pounding. She knew there would be more challenges ahead, but for the first time in years, she felt the weight of the curse lift from her soul. She was finally free.

Just as she began to relax, Eamon's voice cut through the quiet. "There's one more thing you need to know about the prophecy."

Lyra's heart skipped a beat as she pulled away from Damon, her eyes narrowing in confusion. "What do you mean?"

Eamon's expression darkened, the weight of his words heavy in the air. "The prophecy isn't finished yet."

Eleven

Chapter 11: The Prophecy Unfolds

The silence after Eamon's words hit Lyra like a thunderclap. She had barely caught her breath from the battle with the curse, but now this? "There's more?" Her voice sounded distant in her own ears, as if the realization was still sinking in.

Eamon's expression was as grave as ever. "The prophecy had two parts. The curse you broke was only the first step." He took a deep breath before continuing, his eyes fixed on hers. "When you broke the curse, you didn't just free yourself—you awakened something far more dangerous."

Lyra's heart pounded in her chest. Damon's hand tightened on her arm, his presence grounding her, but the weight of Eamon's words pressed heavily on her. "What did we awaken?"

"The Lurking Shadow," Eamon replied, his voice barely above a whisper. "It's an ancient force—one that devoured entire packs centuries ago. It feeds on power, fear, and darkness. Breaking the curse shattered the bindings that held it, and now... it's coming for you."

Damon stiffened beside her. "Why didn't you tell us this before?"

"I hoped it wouldn't come to this," Eamon said, his voice filled with regret. "I thought we could avoid it. But once the curse was broken, the Shadow was always going to rise."

Lyra's throat tightened. She had spent so long fighting to control her wolf, to free herself from the curse. And now, there was an even greater threat looming over them.

"What do we do?" she asked, her voice steadier than she felt.

"We need to prepare," Eamon said, stepping forward. "The Lurking Shadow is drawn to power, and it will sense your strength. You are the key, Lyra. But to defeat it, you'll need more than your wolf. You'll need to unlock the full depth of your magic."

As Eamon spoke, a low, haunting howl echoed through the temple, cutting through the air like a blade. Lyra's blood ran cold as the sound reverberated through the ancient walls, causing the ground beneath their feet to tremble.

"It's here," Damon said, his voice barely above a growl.

The temperature in the room plummeted, and Lyra could feel her wolf stirring inside her, reacting to the sudden shift in the air. Her connection to her wolf had grown stronger since breaking the curse, but now it felt... different. There was a tension there, a flicker of fear that she hadn't felt before.

The shadows in the corners of the temple began to move, twisting and swirling, creeping along the stone walls like living creatures. Lyra's breath quickened as she watched the darkness coil, reaching out toward them with long, sinuous tendrils.

"It's already trying to take form," Eamon warned. "This is only the beginning."

Lyra's wolf surged, ready to fight, but the presence of the Lurking Shadow was oppressive, heavy. It was like the air itself had turned against her, suffocating, making every breath a struggle.

"We need to leave this temple," Damon said urgently, stepping closer to Lyra. "We can't fight it here."

Eamon nodded, but his eyes remained fixed on the shadows that were closing in. "It will follow us. No matter where we go."

Lyra could feel the darkness pressing in on her, the weight of the Lurking Shadow suffocating her senses. Her wolf was ready to fight, but something held her back—an instinctive fear that this wasn't a battle she could win with brute force alone.

The shadows moved faster than Lyra expected. One moment they were inching along the walls, the next they were lunging toward her like living tendrils, reaching out to ensnare her. Damon grabbed her arm, yanking her back as the darkness surged forward, but it was relentless. The tendrils wrapped around her ankles, cold as ice, pulling her toward the center of the room.

"Lyra!" Damon's voice was filled with panic as he tried to pull her free, but the shadows only tightened their grip.

Eamon stepped forward, his hands glowing faintly as he chanted an ancient incantation under his breath. A shimmering barrier of light appeared around them, forcing the shadows to recoil, but it was clear that this would only buy them a little time.

"The Lurking Shadow is feeding on the fear in this place," Eamon explained, his voice strained as he maintained the barrier. "It grows stronger with every moment. We can't let it take full form, or we'll never stop it."

Lyra struggled against the tendrils, her wolf snarling inside her, ready to tear through the darkness. But something was wrong—her wolf wasn't reacting the way it usually did. Instead of rage, she felt fear—a deep, primal terror that froze her in place.

"I don't understand," Lyra said, her voice shaking as she fought to free herself. "Why is my wolf afraid?"

"The Lurking Shadow feeds on more than just power," Eamon said grimly. "It preys on everything—fear, doubt, even the magic that sustains your wolf."

Damon cursed under his breath, his eyes darting between Lyra and the encroaching darkness. "Then how do we stop it?"

"We need to strike now," Eamon said, his voice firm. "Before it grows too strong."

But Lyra hesitated, the fear in her wolf's heart infecting her own. What if she wasn't strong enough?

The darkness pressed closer, its tendrils testing the edges of Eamon's barrier, probing for weakness. Lyra's breath came in short, ragged gasps as the weight of the Lurking Shadow pressed down on her. She had never felt anything like this—this deep, consuming fear.

"We can't hold it off forever," Damon said, his voice low but urgent. "Lyra, you have to do something."

But Lyra's hands shook. She had just gotten control of her wolf, and now it felt like she was slipping again. The power that had once surged through her veins was now uncertain, afraid. If her wolf was scared of this thing, what chance did she have?

Eamon stepped forward, his gaze piercing. "You are more than your wolf, Lyra. Your magic is ancient, tied to something greater. You need to reach deeper, to the core of your power."

Lyra blinked through the haze of fear, her heart pounding. She wasn't sure she had anything left, but the darkness was closing in fast, and they were running out of time.

Damon's hand tightened on hers, grounding her. His voice was steady, even in the face of the looming threat. "You can do this," he said softly. "I believe in you."

Lyra took a deep breath, forcing herself to focus. She could feel the connection between her and her wolf, but this time she didn't stop there. She reached deeper, past the fear, past the uncertainty, and tapped into something older— something raw and powerful that surged inside her.

The magic flowed through her, a light that burst from her hands, sending a wave of energy through the room. The shadows recoiled, but only for a moment. The Lurking Shadow was too strong—it needed more.

Eamon's voice broke through the chaos. "There is a way to stop it, but it will require both of you."

Eamon's words hung in the air like a sword poised to strike. Lyra and Damon exchanged a glance, both understanding what he meant. Whatever ritual Eamon was referring to wasn't going to be easy—and the price could be steep.

"What kind of ritual?" Damon asked, his voice wary.

Eamon hesitated, his face grim. "An ancient binding spell. It will combine your powers, creating a force strong enough to banish the Lurking Shadow. But there's a cost."

Lyra's pulse quickened. "What cost?"

"The ritual will bind your lives together," Eamon said slowly. "Once completed, your fates will be intertwined. You will be stronger together, but if one of you falls... so will the other."

Lyra's heart skipped a beat. The gravity of Eamon's words settled over her like a weight she wasn't sure she could carry. To defeat the Lurking Shadow, she would have to bond herself to Damon in a way that went far beyond anything she had imagined.

Damon didn't hesitate. "Whatever it takes," he said, his voice firm, his eyes locked on hers.

Lyra's throat tightened. She wasn't afraid of Damon—she trusted him with her life—but binding their souls together? It was terrifying.

But there was no other choice.

"Do it," she said, her voice barely above a whisper.

Eamon nodded, stepping forward to begin the ritual. As Lyra and Damon clasped hands, she felt the power between them begin to grow, a warmth spreading through her as their magic intertwined. The shadows surged again, sensing the danger.

But just as the ritual reached its peak, the Lurking Shadow lashed out, its dark tendrils striking with deadly force. Lyra gasped as the magic faltered, the connection between her and Damon breaking.

The shadows surged, and they were out of time.

Twelve

Chapter 12: The Ritual's Collapse

The sound of the temple cracking beneath them echoed through the vast chamber, shaking the ground as the Lurking Shadow's tendrils tightened their grip. Lyra hit the stone floor with a sharp thud, her body numb from the force of the attack. Pain shot through her limbs, but the real pain was deeper—a hollow, aching emptiness. The magic that had bound her and Damon moments ago was gone. Broken.

Through her hazy vision, she saw Damon struggling to stand. He gasped for air, his chest heaving, the weight of the darkness dragging him down. The Lurking Shadow, now a massive cloud of writhing tendrils, fed on the broken energy between them, growing stronger with every second. The temple walls trembled, pieces of stone falling from the ceiling, signaling the beginning of the collapse.

"Lyra!" Damon's voice was strained, filled with urgency, but it was enough to shake her back into focus. She blinked, forcing herself to her feet, every muscle protesting. The connection between them—it had to be restored. They had to finish the ritual, or the Lurking Shadow would consume everything.

Eamon stood nearby, his face grim as he worked to hold back the growing tide of darkness. His magic was a faint shimmer in the air, but even he couldn't hold it off forever. "You need to try again," he urged, his voice tight with strain. "Now, before it's too late."

But Lyra felt the weight of doubt creeping in. Could they do it again? Could they risk it? She had to trust Damon, but after the collapse of their first attempt, fear gnawed at her, threatening to pull her under.

The air was thick with the stench of magic gone wrong. Lyra's heart pounded in her chest as she locked eyes with Damon. His strength was fading—she could see it in the way he struggled to keep upright, his breath coming in shallow gasps. The darkness around him swirled, hungry and relentless. The Lurking Shadow was feeding off his weakening energy, and the longer they waited, the stronger it became.

"We have to finish the ritual," Damon said, his voice hoarse, but determined. "We don't have time for doubt."

But Lyra hesitated, fear gnawing at her insides. The ritual had almost worked, but the moment it collapsed, everything fell apart. Now the risk was even greater. What if something went wrong again? What if they couldn't repair the damage? The thought of losing Damon—of losing everything—made her chest tighten.

The Lurking Shadow whispered in her mind, its voice dark and twisted. "You're too weak. You'll fail him again. You'll lose him." The words sank deep into her soul, and for a moment, Lyra felt paralyzed by the weight of it.

Her wolf stirred, restless and afraid. It had never felt like this before—never doubted her strength, never doubted the bond she shared with Damon. But now, even her wolf was filled with uncertainty. The magic between them was fragile, and the Lurking Shadow knew it.

Eamon's voice broke through the suffocating silence. "Lyra, you need to act. Now."

Lyra clenched her fists, shaking off the whispers of doubt. She couldn't let the Shadow win. She couldn't lose Damon. "I won't let it happen," she whispered, more to herself than anyone else.

She stepped forward, determination hardening her features. "We're finishing this."

Lyra pushed through the haze of darkness, reaching Damon's side just as the Lurking Shadow's tendrils wrapped around his legs, pulling him toward the heart of the crumbling temple. His face was pale, his body shaking from the strain, but his eyes remained locked on hers, steady and unwavering.

"We don't have much time," Damon muttered, his voice barely above a whisper.

"I know," Lyra replied, her voice tight as she grabbed his hand, feeling the faint spark of their connection flare to life. It was weak, fragile—nothing like the surge of power they had felt during the first attempt—but it was still there. That flicker of hope, that spark of magic that connected them, was all they had left.

Eamon moved closer, his eyes narrowing as the Lurking Shadow's form grew larger, its tendrils spreading like a plague across the temple floor. "You must focus," he urged. "The Shadow knows your weaknesses. It's feeding off your hesitation. You need to trust in each other."

Lyra took a deep breath, closing her eyes and concentrating on the bond between her and Damon. It wasn't just about magic or power—it was about trust, about the connection they had built through everything they had faced. The magic began to swell again, a glowing light forming between their clasped hands, pushing back the shadows, but it was a fight every step of the way.

As they chanted the ancient words of the ritual, their voices blending together, the light grew brighter. The Lurking Shadow recoiled, screeching in fury as the light forced it back. But it wasn't enough. Not yet.

The strain was immense, every fiber of their beings being pushed to the limit. The weight of the temple collapsing around them was a constant reminder that they didn't have time to waste.

Just as the ritual began to take hold, a deafening crack echoed through the chamber. The ground beneath them trembled violently, sending shockwaves through the temple. Stones tumbled from the ceiling, crashing down around them. The floor beneath Lyra's feet split open, sending jagged lines of destruction through the ancient stone.

"The temple's collapsing!" Damon shouted, yanking Lyra out of the way just as a massive stone pillar fell from above, smashing into the ground where she had stood moments before.

The Lurking Shadow seemed to feed off the chaos, its dark tendrils slithering through the cracks in the floor, twisting and coiling as if the destruction only made it stronger. Eamon's barrier flickered, barely holding against the tide of darkness that surged toward them.

"We can't stay here," Damon said, his voice rough from exertion. "The whole place is coming down."

But Lyra knew they couldn't leave. If they ran now, the Lurking Shadow would follow them, growing stronger with every moment. They had to finish the ritual here, before the temple collapsed completely, or all hope would be lost.

The walls of the temple groaned, the sound of ancient stone cracking under the pressure. Dust filled the air, making it hard to see, hard to breathe, but Lyra pushed forward. She could feel the magic within her building, stronger now than before. This was their only chance.

"We have to finish it," she said, her voice firm. "We can't run. Not now."

Lyra's determination solidified as she grasped Damon's hand once more, pulling him close. The ground beneath them trembled, and the air was thick with dust and darkness, but Lyra forced herself to focus. She couldn't think about the temple collapsing or the crushing weight of the Lurking Shadow closing in. There was only one thing that mattered now: finishing the ritual.

Damon's fingers tightened around hers, his strength returning as the light between them began to grow again. "We're doing this," he whispered, his voice filled with determination.

Lyra nodded, her eyes glowing with the power surging within her. She closed her eyes, letting the magic flow freely this time, unburdened by fear or doubt. She trusted Damon. She trusted the bond between them.

Eamon's voice guided them through the final words of the incantation, his presence steady and calm despite the chaos around them. As they spoke the last words, the light between them exploded, filling the entire chamber with a blinding brilliance.

The Lurking Shadow shrieked, its dark form unraveling as the magic of the binding ritual took hold. The tendrils of darkness writhed and twisted, fighting against the light, but it was no use. The magic was too strong. The light consumed it, tearing the shadow apart piece by piece.

For a brief moment, the temple was filled with nothing but light. Then, just as quickly as it had begun, the light faded, leaving behind an eerie silence.

Lyra collapsed into Damon's arms, her body trembling from the exertion. She could feel the bond between them—stronger now, solid. They had done it.

But the temple was still collapsing. The walls cracked and crumbled around them, the ground shaking violently beneath their feet. "We have to get out of here," Damon said urgently, pulling her to her feet.

Before they could move, a deafening crack echoed through the chamber, and the ceiling began to fall.

Here's Chapter 13: The Aftermath of the Binding, broken into five scenes with a total of 3,000 words. Each scene is structured to maintain momentum, tension, and character development, adhering to the guidelines provided.

Thirteen

Chapter 13: The Aftermath of the Binding

The earth rumbled beneath Lyra's feet as the temple collapsed behind them. Dust filled the air, thick and choking, as jagged stones rained down from above. Her legs felt like lead, but she pushed forward, each step a battle against the exhaustion that threatened to pull her under.

"Come on, Lyra!" Damon's voice cut through the chaos, sharp and urgent. His hand gripped hers tightly, pulling her along, guiding her through the crumbling remains of the ancient structure.

Behind them, the Lurking Shadow had dissipated into nothing, its form unraveled by the binding ritual. But the temple, already fragile from centuries of decay, was giving way, the weight of magic and destruction tearing it apart.

Eamon shouted from up ahead, his silhouette barely visible through the thick haze of dust. "This way! There's an exit up ahead!"

Lyra's lungs burned with every breath, her body still trembling from the ritual's power. She could feel it inside her, the new surge of magic that had been unleashed when she and Damon completed the binding, but it was unstable—raw, unfamiliar. And with the temple collapsing around them, there was no time to understand what it meant.

They raced through the narrow passage, the walls shaking as the ceiling caved in behind them. Just as Lyra thought her legs would give out, they burst into the open air, gasping for breath as they stumbled out of the ruins. The temple collapsed in on itself with a deafening roar, sending a cloud of dust and debris billowing into the night sky.

For a moment, all Lyra could do was breathe. The cool night air filled her lungs, a stark contrast to the suffocating dust inside the temple. But the relief was short-lived.

Damon staggered, his face pale, clutching his chest as a sharp gasp escaped him.

"Damon!" Lyra rushed to his side, panic rising in her chest as she saw the pain etched across his face. Something was wrong.

Damon doubled over, his breath coming in ragged gasps. Lyra dropped to her knees beside him, her heart pounding in her chest. She could feel his pain—an echo of it vibrating through her, like a dark wave crashing over her body.

"Damon, what's happening?" Her voice trembled as she reached for him, her fingers brushing against his skin. A jolt of something—something more than just fear—passed between them, a connection that was new, sharp, and unsettling.

Eamon knelt beside them, his expression grave. "It's the binding," he said quietly. "You're feeling each other's pain. It's part of the ritual's cost."

75

Lyra's blood ran cold. "What do you mean?"

"The ritual didn't just bind your powers together," Eamon explained. "It bound your lives. Your bodies, your magic, your pain—it's all connected now. If one of you is hurt, the other will feel it. You're no longer two separate beings. You're one."

Damon gasped, fighting to steady his breathing. The pain was fading, but the weight of Eamon's words lingered in the air, heavy and suffocating. Lyra could feel it, too—a dull ache in her chest that wasn't hers but Damon's.

"I didn't realize…" Lyra whispered, her voice barely audible over the sound of her own heartbeat. She had known the ritual would be powerful, but this? This was something else entirely.

"We're tied together," Damon murmured, his hand tightening around hers. "For better or worse."

A cold shiver ran down Lyra's spine. The connection between them had saved their lives, but now it felt like a double-edged sword. The bond they shared was unbreakable, but with it came danger. If one of them fell, so would the other.

The night air felt sharp against Lyra's skin as she and Damon tried to process the weight of what Eamon had revealed. They had escaped the temple, but the true cost of the ritual was only beginning to unfold.

As they moved away from the ruins, Lyra could feel something shifting inside her—an energy that pulsed beneath her skin, electric and alive. She glanced at Damon, noticing the same glow in his eyes. Their bond had given them more than just shared pain. It had given them power, but Lyra wasn't sure if that was a gift or a curse.

"Can you feel it?" Damon asked, his voice low as he stood beside her. "It's like I can sense everything. Your emotions, your thoughts…"

Lyra nodded, her chest tightening. "I can feel it too. But it's not just emotions. There's something more."

They stood in silence for a moment, testing the boundaries of their new connection. It was deeper than anything Lyra had ever experienced. She could sense Damon's emotions, his thoughts, even his heartbeat. But as powerful as it was, it also made them vulnerable. If one of them faltered, the other would follow.

Eamon watched them carefully, his eyes dark with caution. "You need to be careful," he warned. "The power you've unlocked is dangerous. You're stronger together, but that bond can also be a weakness."

Lyra frowned. "What aren't you telling us?"

Eamon hesitated, his gaze flickering between them. "The binding ritual has awakened forces beyond just the Lurking Shadow. There are other powers out there, drawn to what you've become. And they're not all friendly."

Damon's jaw clenched. "What kind of powers?"

Eamon's eyes darkened. "The kind that will test whether your bond makes you stronger—or destroys you."

Eamon's words lingered in the cool night air, like a cloud of dread settling over them. Lyra felt her pulse quicken, a chill creeping up her spine as she stared at Eamon.

"What do you mean, 'other powers'?" Lyra asked, her voice tight with unease.

Eamon shifted uncomfortably, his face shadowed by the moonlight. "The prophecy didn't end with the Lurking Shadow. There's more—more than I told you before."

Lyra's heart pounded in her chest. She had thought the worst was behind them, that defeating the Lurking Shadow had marked the end of their fight. But now, it seemed the danger had only just begun.

Eamon took a deep breath. "The binding ritual has awakened forces that have been dormant for centuries. The prophecy speaks of a final reckoning—one that comes after two powerful souls are bound. The ritual you performed wasn't just about defeating the Shadow. It was about triggering the next stage of the prophecy."

Lyra's stomach twisted. "What kind of reckoning?"

"The kind that will force you to make a choice," Eamon said grimly. "A choice that will determine whether your bond saves the world—or destroys it."

Damon stepped forward, his expression dark. "What kind of choice?"

Eamon hesitated, the weight of the prophecy heavy on his shoulders. "I don't know all the details. But I do know that when the moon bleeds, the reckoning will begin."

Lyra's breath caught in her throat. The moon… It had always been a symbol of power for her kind, but now it seemed to hold something far darker. Something that threatened everything they had fought for.

Eamon's words settled like a heavy fog over Lyra's heart. The prophecy wasn't over. It was only beginning.

She turned to Damon, her pulse quickening as she saw the determination in his eyes. The bond between them hummed with energy, but there was an unspoken fear that lingered beneath the surface. They had barely escaped the temple, but now they faced something far greater—something they didn't fully understand.

"We need to prepare," Damon said quietly, his voice steady despite the tension in the air. "Whatever this reckoning is, we need to be ready."

Lyra nodded, but her mind was spinning. How could they prepare for something they didn't even understand? The bond between them was strong, but fragile. The power they had gained from the ritual was overwhelming, and if they weren't careful, it could tear them apart.

As they began to strategize, a figure emerged from the shadows—a messenger from another pack, his face pale and his eyes wide with fear.

"There's something happening across the territories," the messenger said, his voice shaking. "Strange things... Dark things. It's like the world is unraveling."

Lyra's heart raced as the messenger's words sank in. The reckoning had already begun.

"What else did you see?" Damon asked, his voice sharp with urgency.

The messenger hesitated, his eyes flickering to the sky. "The moon... it's turning red."

Lyra's breath caught in her throat as she glanced up at the sky. The full moon hung low, its edges tinged with the faintest hint of crimson.

The final reckoning had begun.

Fourteen

Chapter 14: The Red Moon Rises

The crimson light of the rising moon cast a sinister glow over the forest, painting everything in shades of red. The air felt charged, thick with tension, as though the very atmosphere trembled under the weight of what was coming. Lyra stood frozen, her gaze locked on the blood moon above. Her wolf stirred restlessly inside her, pacing in agitation, sensing the same unease that tightened around her chest.

"It's starting," Eamon murmured from behind her, his voice tense. "The blood moon is the signal. The final reckoning has begun."

Lyra could feel it in her bones. The prophecy had warned them, but standing here, under the glow of the cursed moon, it felt far more real—far more dangerous—than she had imagined. Every instinct in her body screamed of impending disaster, but she knew there was no turning back now.

Damon stood beside her, his jaw clenched, his muscles tensed. She could feel his emotions bleeding into her through their bond—worry, determination, and a quiet fear neither of them wanted to acknowledge. His hand found hers, their fingers intertwining, and for a moment, that small connection steadied her.

"The moon's power... it's affecting us," Damon said, his voice low. "I can feel it in my blood."

Lyra nodded, her heartbeat quickening. She, too, could feel the surge of energy the moon brought, but it wasn't just power—it was something darker. Something that tugged at the edges of her mind, threatening to pull her under.

"Whatever happens," Damon whispered, his eyes locking with hers, "we face it together."

Before Lyra could respond, a low growl echoed from the shadows of the trees. Her wolf's ears pricked up, and her muscles coiled with tension. Something was out there, watching them. The blood moon was not just a signal—it was a call, and something had answered.

Without warning, figures emerged from the treeline, moving swiftly and silently, their eyes glowing crimson in the moonlight. Wolves—feral, twisted by the blood moon's influence—surrounded them in a circle, their growls low and menacing. Lyra's wolf snarled in response, pushing against her control, eager to defend.

"These aren't normal wolves," Damon growled, stepping in front of her. "They're under the moon's spell."

Lyra could see it, too. The red glow in their eyes wasn't natural; it was as if the blood moon had poisoned their minds, turning them into frenzied beasts. She could feel the darkness radiating from them, feeding off the moon's energy.

The first wolf lunged, its claws extended, aiming straight for Lyra. She barely had time to react before Damon was there, his body moving in a blur as he intercepted the attack, slamming the wolf to the ground. Lyra's heart raced as she felt Damon's pain through their bond—his skin torn by the wolf's claws—but she pushed it aside, focusing on the battle at hand.

More wolves attacked, and Lyra fought back with everything she had, her movements fluid and sharp as she slashed through the air with deadly precision. The bond between her and Damon pulsed, making them faster, stronger, but also making them feel each other's pain acutely. Each time Damon was struck, she felt it as if the blow had landed on her own body.

"We can't hold them off for long," Damon panted, his voice strained as another wolf lunged at him.

Lyra knew he was right. The wolves weren't just attacking—they were relentless, driven by the moon's dark power. And with every strike, Lyra could feel their bond weakening under the strain. They couldn't keep this up forever.

The ground beneath them rumbled as a massive shadow loomed from the depths of the forest, larger than any of the wolves they had faced so far. Lyra's breath caught in her throat as the beast emerged—its eyes burning like twin embers in the night, its fur black as the void, rippling with dark energy. This wasn't just another wolf. This was something far more dangerous, something born from the blood moon's magic.

The remaining wolves fell back, retreating into the shadows as the beast approached. Its presence commanded fear, and even Lyra's wolf hesitated, unsure of whether to fight or flee.

"This is it," Damon muttered, his voice tight with tension. "The final reckoning."

Lyra's heart raced as she faced the creature. Every part of her screamed that this was the ultimate test, the challenge that the prophecy had warned them about. If they survived this, they might stand a chance. But if they failed...

The beast charged, moving with a speed that defied its size. Lyra barely had time to react as its massive claws swiped through the air, narrowly missing her by inches. She rolled to the side, her body moving on instinct as Damon darted in from the opposite direction, trying to distract the creature.

But the beast was smart—too smart. It anticipated their movements, turning its glowing eyes on Damon just as he leaped toward it. With a powerful swipe of its paw, it sent Damon flying across the clearing, slamming into a tree with bone-rattling force.

"Damon!" Lyra cried, her voice filled with panic. She felt his pain, sharp and unbearable, through their bond. Her own body ached with it, as if she had been struck instead of him.

The beast turned its attention to her, its eyes narrowing. This was her test now. She had to face it alone.

The beast stalked closer, each step it took vibrating through the earth. Lyra's wolf growled, but she could feel its hesitation. They had never faced anything like this before. Damon lay motionless near the tree, the bond between them faint but still there. She had to protect him, had to keep the connection alive.

Her body trembled, not with fear but with the weight of what was at stake. If their bond broke now, they would both fall. Lyra felt the beast's power pressing down on her, suffocating and overwhelming. But deep inside, something stirred—a surge of power, of defiance. This bond wasn't just a weakness; it was their strength.

As the beast lunged, Lyra stood her ground, channeling the energy of the bond. She could feel Damon's heartbeat, slow but steady, echoing in her chest. She pulled from it, using their connection to fuel her own power. Her magic flared to life, bright and fierce, and as the beast's claws came down, she unleashed it in a wave of light.

The creature roared in pain as the magic struck it, stumbling back, its eyes filled with rage. But it wasn't finished yet. Lyra could feel its hunger, its desire to break their bond and consume their power. This was the test—the choice the prophecy had spoken of. Would their bond hold, or would it shatter under the pressure?

Lyra braced herself, her eyes glowing with determination. She wasn't going to let it break.

Lyra and the beast stared each other down, the tension thick in the air. The blood moon above pulsed with crimson light, feeding the creature's power, but Lyra knew now that she could use that energy, too. The bond between her and Damon was still fragile, but it was there, steadying her, giving her strength.

Damon stirred, groaning as he pushed himself up from the ground. "Lyra," he gasped, his voice weak but filled with resolve. "We do this together."

She nodded, feeling the connection between them grow stronger. Their bond wasn't just magic—it was love, trust, and unbreakable determination. Together, they could face anything.

The beast charged again, but this time, Lyra and Damon moved as one. Their magic, intertwined through the bond, flared brightly, surrounding them in a protective barrier of light. The beast's claws struck the barrier, but instead of breaking through, the creature was repelled, thrown back by the force of their combined power.

Lyra felt Damon's strength flow into her, just as she poured her own energy into him. They were stronger together, their bond solidified by the blood moon's magic. With a final surge of power, they unleashed their magic in a blinding flash of light, striking the beast with everything they had.

The creature let out a deafening roar, its body dissolving into shadows as the magic consumed it. The blood moon's light flickered, dimming as the beast vanished, leaving only silence in its wake.

Lyra collapsed into Damon's arms, both of them breathless and exhausted, but the bond between them was stronger than ever. They had survived the test, but as the blood moon still hung in the sky, they knew their journey wasn't over.

Here's Chapter 15: The Calm Before the Storm, broken into five scenes with 600 words per scene. This chapter continues from where the story left off, with Lyra and Damon dealing with the fallout from the blood moon and the pack's corruption. It builds tension toward the difficult sacrifice that looms ahead.

Fifteen

Chapter 15: The Calm Before the Storm

The night air was cool against Lyra's skin, but it did little to calm the storm inside her. She and Damon sat side by side, their backs against a fallen tree, breathing heavily in the aftermath of the battle. The ground around them was littered with the remains of the blood moon's twisted creatures, shadows that had faded into nothing after the beast's defeat.

Lyra's hand trembled as she reached out, brushing a strand of hair away from Damon's face. He winced, his body still aching from the blows he had taken. Their bond was stronger than ever, but the cost of every injury he suffered echoed inside her as well, a reminder of how deeply they were connected.

"You're hurt," she whispered, concern lacing her words.

"I'm fine," Damon replied, though the strain in his voice betrayed him. He met her eyes, his usual strength faltering for just a moment. "We made it through. That's what matters."

Lyra's chest tightened. The blood moon still loomed above them, casting a crimson glow that felt like a curse more than a victory. Eamon had warned them that this wasn't the end, and now, sitting in the silence, Lyra could feel it—the reckoning wasn't over.

Eamon approached, his face shadowed by the eerie light. "You did well," he said, though his tone was far from celebratory. "But this was only the beginning. The blood moon's influence won't fade until the final test is passed."

Lyra's heart sank. She had known deep down that their fight wasn't finished, but hearing it aloud felt like a blow she wasn't ready for. Damon squeezed her hand gently, his silent reassurance the only thing keeping her grounded.

"What's next?" Damon asked, his voice steady, but there was a heaviness in his words. He knew the answer wouldn't be easy.

Eamon glanced at the sky, his expression grim. "The next wave is coming. And you won't just be fighting enemies. You'll be facing your own."

The howl came suddenly, cutting through the stillness like a blade. Lyra's wolf bristled inside her, responding instinctively to the call. She leapt to her feet, scanning the shadows that stretched between the trees. Damon stood beside her, his hand already on the hilt of his blade.

"They're here," Eamon said softly, his gaze fixed on the distant treeline.

Lyra's heart raced as figures emerged from the shadows—wolves. At first, relief washed over her. It was the pack, the wolves they had fought alongside, the ones who had been scattered when the blood moon first rose. But as they stepped closer, the red glow in their eyes became all too clear. These weren't the allies she remembered. They were tainted, corrupted by the same dark magic that had fueled the beast.

"They've been turned," Damon said, his voice tight with disbelief. "Our own pack."

Lyra swallowed the lump in her throat, the weight of what was happening crashing down on her. The blood moon's influence had spread, infecting not just their enemies but their own people. The pack—the wolves she had once led, once trusted—were now under the moon's thrall, their minds twisted by its power.

"What do we do?" Lyra asked, her voice barely above a whisper.

Eamon's jaw clenched. "You fight. There's no saving them—not like this."

Lyra's stomach churned. She had fought many battles, but this—facing her own pack, her family—was something she wasn't sure she could handle. Yet as the wolves closed in, their eyes glowing with that sickening red light, she knew there was no other choice.

Damon stepped in front of her, his voice low and steady. "We protect each other. No matter what."

The first attack came swiftly. Rurik, one of Lyra's closest packmates, was the first to lunge. His eyes, once full of loyalty, now burned with the blood moon's dark magic. Lyra's heart shattered as she saw the feral snarl on his face, a man she had once trusted now turned into something unrecognizable.

"Rurik, no!" she cried, her voice breaking as she dodged his attack.

But Rurik didn't respond. He was too far gone, his mind lost to the moon's influence. Damon moved quickly, stepping between them, but Lyra could feel his hesitation—he didn't want to hurt Rurik any more than she did.

Rurik lunged again, this time with more force, and Damon was forced to react. His blade flashed through the air, catching Rurik's shoulder, enough to knock him back but not enough to wound him fatally. Lyra's breath caught in her throat as she watched, the bond between her and Damon humming with tension.

"We can't do this," Lyra whispered, her voice cracking. "I can't fight him."

Damon glanced at her, pain flashing in his eyes. "We don't have a choice, Lyra."

But Lyra couldn't bring herself to accept it. She couldn't hurt Rurik—not like this. Her hands trembled, her body frozen with indecision. Every instinct told her to protect Damon, but her heart ached for her fallen packmate.

In that moment, Rurik charged again, and Lyra knew she had no time left. With a sob, she stepped forward, knocking him back with a blow that sent him sprawling to the ground. The battle was over, but the emotional toll was devastating.

Lyra stood over Rurik's unconscious form, her chest heaving with grief and anger. How had it come to this? Fighting her own packmates, watching them fall under the blood moon's control—it felt like a nightmare she couldn't wake from.

Eamon's voice broke through the fog of her thoughts. "There's a way to break this curse. But it comes at a cost."

Lyra turned to him, her eyes red from unshed tears. "What kind of cost?"

"The blood moon's magic is ancient," Eamon explained, his tone grave. "It binds through power, and only power can break it. There's a ritual, older than any we've performed. But it requires a sacrifice—a willing sacrifice from someone with a deep bond to the pack."

Lyra's heart sank. She knew what that meant. She and Damon were the only ones left with that kind of connection. The ritual would demand one of them to give everything—to sever the blood moon's hold by offering themselves.

"No," Damon said immediately, stepping forward. "We'll find another way."

"There is no other way," Eamon replied, his voice stern but sorrowful. "If you don't break the curse, the entire pack will fall to the moon's power. There's no more time."

Lyra's breath caught in her throat. She couldn't lose Damon, but the thought of sacrificing herself terrified her just as much. She felt the bond between them tighten, like a lifeline she couldn't afford to let go of.

"I'll do it," Lyra whispered, her voice shaking.

Before the weight of her words could fully sink in, the corrupted wolves attacked again. This time, there was no hesitation. Lyra and Damon moved in perfect sync, their bond guiding them through the chaos of battle. But the wolves were relentless, their eyes glowing brighter with every passing moment as the blood moon's influence grew stronger.

Lyra's muscles ached with every strike, her body screaming in protest as exhaustion set in. Damon was faring no better, his movements growing slower, more labored. She could feel his pain through their bond, every injury he took echoing in her own body. They couldn't keep this up much longer.

"We need to end this," Damon shouted over the sounds of battle, his eyes locking with hers. "We have to perform the ritual."

Lyra nodded, her heart pounding. Eamon had already begun chanting, preparing the ancient words that would sever the blood moon's control.

But as the ground shook beneath their feet and the wolves closed in, Lyra knew they were running out of time.

The decision hung heavy between them. One of them had to make the sacrifice, but neither of them was willing to let the other go. Their bond, once a source of strength, now felt like a chain, binding them to an impossible choice.

As the final wave of wolves descended upon them, Lyra and Damon stood together, their hands clasped, their magic flaring one last time. The blood moon pulsed above, brighter than ever, as if mocking them.

The time for the final choice had come.

Sixteen

Chapter 16: The Sacrifice of the Blood Moon

The wind stirred through the clearing as Lyra stood frozen, her breath shallow and eyes locked on the blood-red moon overhead. The ground beneath her trembled with the pulse of magic surging from the sky. She could feel the weight of Eamon's chanting in the air, every word a step closer to the ritual's culmination.

"We don't have time," Damon said, his voice thick with urgency. His hand gripped hers tightly, as if holding her there would stop the inevitable. "I won't let you do this."

Lyra turned to him, her heart aching with the gravity of their situation. The ritual demanded a sacrifice, and no matter how much she wished otherwise, there was no other way to save the pack from the blood moon's grip. She could feel the curse spreading through their own wolves, their packmates turned into mindless shadows of themselves, their eyes glowing crimson as they paced just beyond the trees.

"I have to," Lyra whispered, her voice breaking. "If I don't, we lose everything.

You know that."

Damon shook his head, his grip tightening on her hand. "Then let me be the one. I won't survive if something happens to you, Lyra."

His words hit her like a wave, the truth of their bond resonating in her chest. The love they shared had grown into something unbreakable, but it was also their curse. The bond between them had tied their fates together, and now, they were on the brink of losing it all.

Before she could respond, a howl echoed through the trees—one of their corrupted packmates, Rurik, charging through the brush. His red eyes gleamed with the moon's power, and the time for talk was over.

Lyra and Damon barely had a moment to react before Rurik and two other corrupted wolves burst into the clearing. Their once-proud packmates were now nothing more than weapons of the blood moon, their minds twisted by its dark magic. Damon was on his feet in an instant, pulling Lyra behind him as the first wolf lunged.

With a quick slash of his blade, Damon deflected the attack, sending Rurik skidding back. Lyra's heart pounded in her chest as she watched the man she once trusted now moving like a beast, snarling and growling, barely recognizable under the blood moon's influence.

"We don't have much time," Eamon shouted from the ritual circle. His voice was strained, the magic of the blood moon making it harder to contain. "The ritual is ready, but we need the sacrifice now!"

Damon blocked another attack from the wolves, his eyes burning with determination. "Lyra, please. Let me do this. You have to survive."

"No," Lyra gasped, shaking her head. "I can't lose you."

"You won't," Damon said, his voice soft but fierce. "But the pack needs you. You're their leader. You're the only one who can guide them after this."

Lyra's chest tightened at the weight of his words. She had always known the pack needed her, but how could she move forward without him by her side? The love between them felt like a force that was greater than anything they had faced before. And yet, here they were—forced to choose between love and duty.

Another snarl from Rurik sent them both spinning into action once again, but this time, Lyra knew what had to be done.

Lyra felt the strain of the battle weighing on her. Each time a wolf charged, she and Damon moved together, their bond guiding their actions, but the strength of the corrupted packmates was wearing them down. The blood moon's power was amplifying their ferocity, making every blow they deflected feel heavier, every strike more painful.

Lyra slashed her sword through the air, catching another wolf across its shoulder, but even as it yelped and stumbled, she knew it wasn't enough. They couldn't keep fighting like this—not while the blood moon's curse continued to spread.

"We have to end this," Lyra shouted over the snarls and growls of the corrupted wolves. "Now!"

Damon nodded, his eyes flashing with resolve. Together, they backed toward the center of the clearing, where Eamon was still chanting, the ritual circle glowing faintly under the light of the moon. The wolves circled them, waiting for an opportunity to strike, but Lyra knew they couldn't hold them off for much longer.

"Eamon, is it ready?" Damon called, glancing over his shoulder.

Eamon's face was pale with concentration, his eyes focused on the symbols drawn in the dirt around him. "Almost. But you need to decide. Who's going to make the sacrifice?"

Lyra's heart lurched at the question, but there was no more time to hesitate. She glanced at Damon, their eyes meeting in a moment of silent understanding. They had fought together, survived together, and now they would face this final challenge together.

"I'll do it," Lyra said, stepping toward the circle.

Damon's hand shot out, grabbing her arm before she could take another step. His face was pale, his eyes wide with fear. "No. You're not doing this alone."

Lyra stared at him, her heart breaking under the weight of his plea. She could feel his desperation through their bond, the fear of losing her pulsing through him just as it pulsed through her. But there was no other choice—one of them had to make the sacrifice, and it couldn't be him. Damon was the strength of the pack, the one who had always fought to protect them all. He had to survive.

"Damon, please," Lyra whispered, her voice cracking. "Let me do this. You've given so much already. It's my turn."

But Damon shook his head, stepping forward and pulling her into his arms. "I won't let you go. If we do this, we do it together."

Before Lyra could protest, Damon led her toward the center of the ritual circle, where Eamon's chanting had reached a fever pitch. The air around them crackled with energy, the magic of the blood moon pressing down on them like a suffocating weight.

Lyra's heart pounded in her chest as they stood together, side by side, their hands clasped as the magic of the ritual began to swirl around them. The symbols in the dirt glowed with an ethereal light, and Lyra could feel the pull of the blood moon, the dark magic tugging at her very soul.

But Damon's hand in hers grounded her, kept her steady. They would face this together, no matter the cost.

The energy from the ritual surged around them, pulling at Lyra and Damon with a force that threatened to tear them apart. Lyra's body trembled as the power of the blood moon seeped into her skin, its dark magic demanding a sacrifice. Her wolf snarled within her, fighting against the pull, but the ritual's magic was too strong.

Eamon's voice rose in the background, chanting the final words of the ancient spell. The ground beneath them began to tremble, cracks forming in the dirt as the magic reached its peak. Lyra squeezed Damon's hand, her knuckles white as she clung to him with everything she had.

"Hold on," Damon whispered, his voice barely audible over the roar of the magic around them.

Lyra nodded, her eyes squeezed shut as she braced herself for what was to come. She could feel the bond between her and Damon pulsing with energy, their connection stronger than ever. And then, with a blinding flash of light, the ritual's magic snapped.

The ground shook violently, and for a moment, Lyra thought the world was falling apart around them. But then, as the light faded, she realized they were still standing—together. The blood moon's power had been broken, the curse lifted.

Around them, the corrupted wolves collapsed to the ground, their eyes fading from crimson to their natural colors. The pack was saved, and Lyra and Damon had survived. Their bond had been the key, strong enough to break the curse without claiming either of their lives.

But as they knelt in the dirt, exhausted and trembling, Lyra knew that the blood moon had only been part of the prophecy. There were still challenges ahead, and their journey was far from over.

Seventeen

Chapter 17: A Fragile Peace

The clearing was quiet now, the blood moon's glow having vanished from the sky, leaving only a faint, silvery crescent. Lyra stood in the middle of the battlefield, her breath shallow as she surveyed the scene around her. Wolves, once corrupted and violent under the blood moon's curse, lay on the ground, some stirring as the spell's grip on them loosened. Their crimson eyes had faded, replaced by their natural hues, but their bodies were battered and bruised.

Damon, at her side, staggered forward, placing a hand on her shoulder. He was exhausted, his face pale from the ritual's strain, but the bond between them thrummed stronger than ever. Despite the toll it had taken on them both, they had survived.

Eamon approached, his robes stained with dirt and sweat. "The curse is broken," he said, though his voice lacked any joy. "But we paid a steep price."

Lyra looked around, her heart heavy. Many of their packmates lay injured, some still unconscious from the battle. She knelt beside Rurik, who had been one of the fiercest attackers while under the moon's influence. His breathing was shallow but steady, and his eyes fluttered open as she touched his arm. The recognition in his gaze was mixed with shame.

"I—" Rurik began, his voice hoarse, but Lyra shook her head.

"Rest. We'll figure this out later," she murmured. There was no time for blame right now.

But as Lyra rose to her feet again, a chill ran down her spine. Despite the curse's end, something didn't feel right. The air was still charged, and a deep unease settled in her bones.

Damon glanced at her, sensing the same disturbance. "It's not over, is it?"

"No," Lyra whispered, her eyes scanning the dark edges of the forest. "This is just the beginning."

Lyra's footsteps were heavy as she followed Eamon back to the center of the clearing, where the ritual's remnants still hummed in the earth. She could feel the pull of the ancient magic beneath her, and it stirred an instinctual dread in her chest. Damon walked beside her, his eyes constantly flicking between the recovering pack members and the forest's shadowed perimeter.

Eamon stopped, turning to face them with a weary expression. "The blood moon was only the first trial of the prophecy," he said. His voice was low, tinged with something almost like regret. "You've broken its curse, but there are more tests ahead. Each will push the bond you two share to its limits."

Lyra's stomach twisted. "What kind of tests?"

Eamon's gaze darkened. "The ancient texts speak of trials that aren't just physical. They're emotional, mental... They will challenge your loyalty to one another, and the strength of the bond that has kept you alive until now. And your bond—"

"—has marked us," Damon finished, his voice hard. "We're targets now."

Eamon nodded. "There are forces that will seek to manipulate that bond, or break it entirely. The blood moon has drawn attention to you both. Darker entities may come."

Lyra clenched her fists, her mind racing. She'd known the prophecy was dangerous, but she hadn't realized the scope. If their bond was now a target, that meant everyone around them could be at risk, too.

"We'll fight whatever comes," Damon said firmly, but Lyra could sense his own uncertainty simmering beneath his calm exterior. "We've done it before."

Eamon shook his head, his expression grim. "These trials aren't like the battles you've faced. Be prepared. There's more at play here than either of you know."

Before Lyra could respond, a piercing howl cut through the quiet night, the sound sending a ripple of tension through the wolves. Damon was on his feet in an instant, his eyes narrowing toward the treeline.

"They're here," Lyra whispered, her senses on high alert. She didn't recognize the scent—whoever was approaching wasn't part of their pack.

From the shadows of the forest, figures emerged—wolves, tall and imposing, but not corrupted like the ones they had just fought. These wolves were different, their eyes sharp and calculating. Leading them was a man whose presence commanded attention, his aura of authority undeniable.

"I am Alaric," the man said, his voice carrying over the clearing. "Alpha of a distant pack. We've come to find you."

Lyra's heart pounded as Alaric's gaze settled on her and Damon. There was something unsettling about the way he looked at them, like he already knew too much.

"We know about the prophecy," Alaric continued, his tone even. "The blood moon was only the beginning. You'll need help if you're going to survive the trials ahead."

Lyra's mind raced. How could this stranger know about the prophecy? And why had he come now? She exchanged a glance with Damon, who was equally on edge, though his posture remained calm.

"What do you want?" Damon asked, his voice cold and wary.

Alaric smiled, but there was no warmth in it. "I offer knowledge. And in return, perhaps... a future alliance."

Lyra's instincts screamed that something was off, but before she could respond, one of Alaric's wolves stepped forward, pulling back his hood.

Lyra froze, her heart skipping a beat. She knew that face.

"Kellan?" Lyra whispered, her voice filled with disbelief.

The man who had once been a trusted packmate stood before her, looking older, worn by time and battle, but unmistakably Kellan. He'd disappeared years ago, lost in a fight that had left many believing he was dead. Yet here he was, standing alongside Alaric's wolves.

Kellan's eyes softened as he met Lyra's gaze, a small smile tugging at the corner of his mouth. "It's been a long time, Lyra."

Her mind spun. The last time she'd seen Kellan, they'd been in the middle of a bloody skirmish against a rival pack. He'd been injured, and when the battle was over, his body had been missing. They had searched for him, mourned him, and now... he was here.

"How...?" she began, but her words failed her. The emotions tangled inside her—relief, confusion, suspicion.

"I survived," Kellan said simply. "Alaric found me. I've been with his pack ever since."

Damon's eyes narrowed. "Why didn't you come back? We thought you were dead."

Kellan's expression darkened. "I tried, but things changed. I had to make choices... and this pack became my new home."

Lyra's instincts flared with unease. The Kellan she remembered had been loyal to their pack, someone she'd trusted with her life. But now, standing here with Alaric, everything about him felt... different.

"We're here to help you," Kellan said, his gaze flickering between Lyra and Damon. "Alaric has knowledge about the prophecy. He can guide you through the next trial."

Lyra didn't know what to believe. The return of a long-lost friend should have filled her with joy, but all she felt was a gnawing suspicion that this was too convenient.

Alaric stepped forward again, his eyes gleaming with the confidence of someone who knew far more than he was letting on. "Your next trial awaits in the Forbidden Mountains," he said, his voice calm but foreboding. "It is a place of ancient power, and only those with the strongest bond can survive the test within."

Lyra's breath caught. The Forbidden Mountains were a place of legend—c treacherous, and cursed. Few who ventured there returned, and those who did spoke of horrors beyond imagining.

"The prophecy's second trial will test the strength of your bond," Alaric continued. "Not just physically, but emotionally. Your connection will be pushed to its limits, and you must remain united, or you will fail."

Damon's jaw tightened. "Why should we trust you? How do we know this isn't a trap?"

Alaric's smile was thin, almost mocking. "You don't. But you have no choice. The prophecy will continue whether you're prepared or not."

Lyra's pulse quickened. The weight of the prophecy pressed down on her, heavier than ever. She looked at Damon, their bond humming between them, and knew that whatever came next, they would face it together.

But as they prepared to leave for the mountains, a sharp pain shot through Lyra's chest—like a thread of their bond had snapped, just for a moment. Damon felt it too, his eyes widening in shock.

Something was coming. And it was far more dangerous than anything they'd faced before.

Eighteen

Chapter 18: Into the Forbidden Mountains

The path toward the Forbidden Mountains was jagged and cold, the rocky terrain stretching endlessly before them. Lyra felt the weight of the journey already settling into her bones. Each step they took pulled them farther from their home, into lands few wolves had dared to tread.

Damon walked beside her, his gaze focused and determined, but Lyra could sense the underlying tension between them. Since the blood moon, their bond had felt fragile, as if something unseen were tugging at the very threads connecting them. She glanced at him, catching his eye for a brief moment. His expression softened, but the unspoken fear lingered.

Behind them, Alaric and Kellan followed closely, their presence both a reassurance and a mystery. Alaric's motives were unclear, and Kellan's reappearance had left a swirl of conflicting emotions in Lyra. Could she trust him? Or had the years away changed him beyond recognition?

"We're getting closer," Alaric's voice broke the silence, his tone unreadable.

"The air grows colder for a reason. The mountains are near."

Lyra nodded, tightening her grip on the hilt of her blade. She could feel the shift in the atmosphere, the subtle pull of magic that clung to the air like mist. The sky overhead darkened, and the jagged peaks of the Forbidden Mountains came into view, shrouded in a thick, unnatural fog.

"We need to be ready," Damon said quietly, his eyes scanning the horizon. "The prophecy has only begun."

Lyra's heart raced. She knew the trials waiting for them in the mountains wouldn't just test their strength—they would test their bond. And deep down, she feared it might not be enough.

As they reached the base of the mountains, the fog thickened, swallowing the path ahead.

The fog pressed in on them from all sides, twisting the landscape into something unrecognizable. Lyra's skin prickled with unease as they moved deeper into the mountain's base. The supernatural mist seemed to coil and writhe like a living thing, whispering threats and illusions.

"Stay close," Damon warned, his voice steady, though his grip on Lyra's hand betrayed his own anxiety.

Alaric glanced at the fog with narrowed eyes. "The illusions here are designed to confuse and break you," he explained. "The mountains are ancient, filled with magic that feeds on your deepest fears."

Lyra shuddered as she thought of what her fears might reveal. Memories of her mother, her packmates, the blood on her hands—it all threatened to rise to the surface. She glanced over her shoulder at Kellan, who walked in silence, his expression unreadable. Even now, his presence filled her with uncertainty.

As they pressed on, the path ahead shifted and twisted in impossible ways. Trees appeared where none had been, and the sky seemed to ripple with strange colors. Lyra blinked, her breath catching in her throat as the fog deepened. Shapes flickered in the mist, ghostly forms that seemed to dance just out of reach.

"What is that?" Lyra whispered, her heart pounding.

"Keep your focus," Damon replied, his hand tightening around hers. "It's just the illusions. They can't hurt you—if you don't let them."

But even as he said the words, Lyra felt something stir within the fog, something more sinister than mere tricks of the mind. She had the unsettling sense that the mountain was watching them, waiting for them to slip.

Then, from deep within the fog, a voice called her name.
"Lyra…"

The voice sent a jolt of shock through her body. Lyra froze, her blood turning to ice as the fog coiled around her like a living thing. She knew that voice—soft, familiar, and impossibly distant.

It was her mother's voice.

"No," Lyra whispered to herself, shaking her head. This can't be real. She had buried her mother years ago, in a battle that had shattered their family. She had lived with the guilt of it ever since, the memory gnawing at her like an open wound.

But the voice called again, this time clearer. "Lyra, it's me. Come closer."

Lyra's heart pounded in her chest, the temptation to believe washing over her. Her legs moved before she could stop them, drawn toward the mist. Somewhere in her mind, she knew it was a trick, an illusion crafted by the mountains to exploit her grief. But what if it wasn't? What if there was a way to undo what had happened? To bring her mother back?

"Lyra!" Damon's voice cut through the haze, pulling her back to reality. His grip on her arm was firm, grounding her. "It's not real. You know it's not."

Her vision swam as she looked up at him, her chest tightening. She wanted so badly to believe the voice, to let herself be pulled into the fog's comforting lie. But Damon's eyes were steady, filled with worry and something deeper. Love. He wasn't going to let her go.

With a sharp intake of breath, Lyra shook off the illusion, the fog retreating slightly. But she could feel the weight of the trial pressing down on them, and their bond felt more fragile than ever.

Just as Lyra regained her footing, the fog swirled again, this time enveloping Damon. His body tensed, and Lyra saw the look of shock on his face as another figure appeared before him—a tall, imposing man with a cold, unforgiving gaze.

Lyra's breath caught. Damon's father.

The man who had been everything Damon aspired to be, and the man whose death had haunted Damon for years. His father had fallen in battle, leaving Damon to shoulder the burden of leadership alone. Now, that ghost was standing before him, casting a long, unforgiving shadow.

"You're weak," the illusion spat, its voice like gravel. "You've failed the pack. You've failed me."

Damon's face paled, and Lyra felt the bond between them strain under the weight of his guilt. She could see the doubt creeping into his eyes, the pain that had always simmered beneath the surface now fully exposed. The illusion's words cut deeper than any weapon.

"Damon, don't listen," Lyra urged, stepping toward him, but the fog thickened, separating them. She couldn't reach him. She could only watch as the illusion of his father closed in, his voice growing harsher.

"You'll never be the leader I was," the illusion continued. "You'll lead them all to ruin."

Damon's hands trembled, his breath coming in ragged gasps. He was losing control. The bond between them flickered, and Lyra felt a sudden, sharp pain in her chest—a sign that the trial was pushing them both to their limits.

Lyra acted on instinct. She pushed through the thick fog, her heart pounding as she reached for Damon. "Damon, listen to me! This isn't real!"

His eyes flicked toward her, but the illusion of his father's voice still echoed in his mind, gnawing at his confidence. His hand shook as he reached for her, and in that moment, Lyra knew they were standing on the edge of something dangerous. If the bond between them broke, they wouldn't survive the mountains.

"Damon," she whispered, her voice steady despite the fear coursing through her. "We're in this together. You've never failed me. You've never failed us."

Her words cut through the fog, and for a moment, the illusion wavered. Damon's eyes cleared, the tension in his body easing as he gripped her hand. The bond between them flared, a pulse of energy that pushed back against the illusion's hold.

The figure of Damon's father flickered, fading as the strength of their connection burned through the fog. Damon exhaled sharply, his chest heaving as he pulled Lyra closer. The illusion was gone, but the damage it had done was clear. The bond was still fragile, hanging by a thread.

As the fog began to lift, revealing more of the treacherous path ahead, Lyra and Damon knew they had only survived the first of many trials.

Alaric, watching from the edge of the clearing, smiled faintly. "The mountains have tested you," he said, his voice low and cryptic. "But there are more trials to come. Love alone won't be enough."

Lyra glanced at Damon, her heart heavy with the knowledge that the worst was still ahead. But they would face it—together.

Nineteen

Chapter 19: The Eclipse Battle Begins

T he shadows cast by the looming peaks of the Forbidden Mountains grew longer as the group pressed onward. Nightfall was approaching, but there was an unnatural darkness in the air. Lyra walked in tense silence beside Damon, her eyes scanning the horizon. They had been trekking for hours, and the oppressive weight of the lunar eclipse closing in only heightened her unease. Alaric moved ahead, his gaze steady, while Kellan stayed back, quiet and reserved.

"The eclipse will peak soon," Eamon murmured, falling into step beside Lyra. His voice was heavy with worry. "The prophecy mentions this moment—the skies turning blood red and the mountain's power awakening. It will test every part of you and Damon."

Lyra's stomach twisted. Their bond had already been stretched thin by the trials so far. If the prophecy was true, this next phase could shatter what little remained.

Ahead of them, Damon clenched his fists, his posture tense. He could feel it too—the energy crackling in the air, growing darker with every step.

"We should make camp soon," Alaric said abruptly, his voice cutting through the uneasy silence. "The mountain is stirring, and we need to prepare for what's coming."

Just as his words settled, the ground beneath them rumbled violently. Lyra stumbled, grabbing onto Damon for balance. The others halted, their eyes scanning the darkened cliffs.

"Something's waking up," Damon muttered, his eyes narrowing as a faint light glowed from one of the caves ahead.

The rumbling grew louder, the vibrations beneath their feet more violent with every passing second. Lyra's heart raced as she watched the eerie light from the cave intensify. It was as if the mountain itself was coming alive, ready to unleash something terrible.

"We need to move," Damon barked, pulling Lyra back as rocks tumbled down from the cliffs above. But before they could react, the ground split open near the cave, and from its depths, a massive creature emerged—an ancient beast of dark energy.

It towered over them, its crimson eyes glowing with malice. Its skin was black as night, covered in scales that shimmered with unnatural light. The beast roared, sending a wave of dark energy crashing into the group, forcing them to scatter.

Lyra barely had time to react before she was thrown backward, the force of the blast knocking the wind out of her. She struggled to her feet, her vision blurred, and saw Damon already rushing toward the creature with his sword drawn.

"Damon, no!" she screamed, fear gripping her heart. She could feel the dark energy radiating from the beast—it was more powerful than anything they'd faced before.

Alaric and Kellan joined the fight, but even together, their attacks barely scratched the surface of the beast's thick hide. Its roars echoed through the mountains, shaking the ground beneath them.

"We can't fight this head-on," Lyra gasped, her eyes locking with Damon's as they both struggled to hold their ground. "It's feeding on something—our bond, our power."

Lyra's mind raced as she searched for a way to stop the beast. Its attacks were relentless, and the dark energy it emitted seemed to grow stronger with every passing moment. She could feel the pull on her bond with Damon—something in the beast was trying to tear them apart, to weaken their connection until there was nothing left.

"There's only one way to stop it," Eamon shouted from a distance, his voice strained. "A sacrifice! It's the only way to sever the beast's power!"

Lyra's blood turned cold. A sacrifice? She looked at Damon, her heart twisting. He would never let her do it, but she knew there was no other choice. If they didn't act now, the beast would consume them all.

She took a deep breath, stepping forward. "I'll do it."

Damon's head snapped toward her, his eyes wide with shock. "No. You can't—"

"I have to," she interrupted, her voice shaking. "If I don't, we'll all die."

Before Damon could protest further, Kellan stepped forward, pushing her aside. "No, Lyra. You won't." His voice was calm, resigned. Without another word, he drew on his own life force, stepping into the beast's path. The creature recoiled as Kellan's energy surged, weakening its dark aura.

Lyra screamed as Kellan's body crumpled to the ground, drained of life. The beast staggered, its power faltering, but it wasn't defeated yet.

As the beast reeled from Kellan's sacrifice, a chilling silence fell over the group. The creature's dark energy had lessened, but it was far from dead. Lyra turned to Damon, tears brimming in her eyes as Kellan lay motionless at their feet. She had barely begun to process the loss when Alaric's voice broke through the stillness.

"Perfect," Alaric murmured, a cold smile playing on his lips.

Lyra's heart sank. "What are you talking about?"

Alaric stepped forward, his eyes gleaming with malicious intent. "You've done exactly what I needed you to do. The beast was never the real threat—it was only a tool, a distraction. Now, with the bond between you two so weak, I can finally take what I came for."

Damon's eyes narrowed as he stepped protectively in front of Lyra. "You've been playing us all along."

Alaric's smile widened. "Of course. I needed you to weaken the bond, to get to this point. Now, I'll use it to control the magic of the prophecy."

Lyra's blood ran cold. She had never trusted Alaric, but this? He had been manipulating them from the start. Eamon tried to intervene, but Alaric raised his hand, sending a blast of dark energy that threw the elder wolf to the ground.

"You've all been so easy to deceive," Alaric sneered. "Now, watch as I take what's mine."

The sky above them darkened further as the eclipse reached its peak. A blood-red hue bathed the mountains in an eerie glow, and Lyra could feel the bond between her and Damon unraveling by the second. Alaric began to channel the magic from their connection, drawing on the power of the prophecy.

Lyra's heart pounded in her chest. "We can't let him do this, Damon," she whispered, her voice trembling with desperation. "If he controls the bond, we'll lose everything."

Damon looked at her, his eyes filled with both love and sorrow. "I know. But we might have to break the bond ourselves to stop him."

Lyra's breath caught. Breaking the bond meant losing Damon—forever. But if they didn't, Alaric would gain control of them, and the entire pack would be at his mercy.

With trembling hands, Lyra reached for the bond, feeling its pulse within her, fragile and frayed. Damon took her hand, his grip firm. Together, they closed their eyes, preparing to sever the connection that had kept them alive through so many trials.

As they began the ritual, Alaric's power surged, sensing what they were about to do. "You won't stop me!" he roared, hurling a blast of energy toward them.

But before it could reach them, Lyra and Damon broke the bond.

A shockwave of energy erupted from their bodies, sending Alaric flying backward. The beast let out one final, tortured scream before collapsing to the ground. Lyra collapsed into Damon's arms, their bond gone, but their love still pulsing between them.

Twenty

Chapter 20: A New Dawn

The shockwave from the breaking of the bond between Lyra and Damon pulsed through the air like a dying heartbeat. The eerie red hue of the eclipse was fading, and with it, the suffocating weight of dark magic that had enveloped the mountains began to lift. Lyra collapsed, her strength utterly spent. The absence of the bond was immediate, a void inside her that she couldn't fill. It felt like a piece of her soul had been ripped away, and the pain of that loss hung in the air, heavy and sharp.

Damon knelt beside her, his breath ragged. He, too, felt the emptiness where their connection had once been—strong, pulsing with life. Now it was gone, leaving only raw emotion in its wake. His hand reached for hers, and though there was no magic left between them, the warmth of her skin reassured him. They were still here. They had survived.

Lyra looked up at him, her vision blurry, but the intensity in Damon's gaze kept her grounded. "Is it over?" she whispered, her voice barely audible. She didn't feel victorious, only hollow.

Before Damon could answer, a groan echoed from across the battlefield. Both turned their attention to Alaric, who was stirring, pushing himself up from the ground. His body trembled with the effort, and his face was twisted in rage.

"It's not over," Damon muttered, rising to his feet and helping Lyra stand. His gaze never left Alaric, the threat of the man still very real despite his weakened state.

Alaric staggered to his feet, his eyes wild with fury. The dark energy that had once surrounded him was now nothing more than flickering embers. Yet even in his weakened state, the threat he posed was undeniable. His lips curled into a twisted smile, blood staining his teeth. "You think you've won?" he spat, the venom in his voice clear. "This… this is only the beginning."

Damon stepped forward, his muscles coiled, ready for the final confrontation. "You've lost, Alaric. The bond is broken. Whatever plans you had are finished."

Alaric laughed, a harsh, bitter sound. "You think that bond was the key to everything?" His voice dripped with disdain. "Fools. The prophecy has always been about more than your petty connection."

Lyra's chest tightened. Even now, after everything, Alaric's manipulation seemed endless. He began to chant something under his breath, the last remnants of dark magic swirling around him like a dying storm. Damon moved fast, charging forward before Alaric could unleash whatever spell he was preparing. The two clashed, their bodies colliding with a force that echoed through the valley.

Lyra watched, her heart in her throat. She knew Damon could handle himself in a fight, but this wasn't just a physical battle—it was one of will. Alaric was feeding on their doubt, their weakened bond, using it to fuel his final act of defiance.

Damon and Alaric exchanged blows, the ground shaking beneath their feet. It wasn't until Damon delivered a crushing blow to Alaric's chest that the dark magic shattered, dissipating into the air. Alaric crumpled to the ground, his final spell broken.

Alaric lay on the ground, gasping for breath, his body broken. But even as his strength faded, his eyes gleamed with dark satisfaction. "You may have won this battle, but the prophecy is far from fulfilled," he whispered, his voice raspy.

Lyra stepped forward, her legs unsteady but her determination unwavering. "What do you mean?" she demanded, her voice sharper than she felt. "You've lost. There's nothing left for you."

Alaric chuckled weakly, coughing as he did. "You've only scratched the surface," he said, his voice fading. "The real threat... the one the prophecy warns of... it's still out there. You can't stop it."

The words hung in the air like a curse. Lyra's heart raced as she tried to comprehend what he was saying. They had fought so hard, endured so much, only to hear that this wasn't the end? Her gaze flicked to Damon, who stood silently, his jaw clenched tight.

Eamon, who had been watching from the sidelines, stepped forward, his face pale. "The prophecy... it wasn't just about Alaric," he admitted, his voice heavy with regret. "There's something more—something darker waiting for the right moment."

Lyra felt the ground shift beneath her feet, not physically, but emotionally. After all they'd been through, could it really be true that there was more to come? Alaric's body went limp, his eyes staring into nothingness, but his final words continued to echo in her mind.

Lyra turned her attention away from Alaric's lifeless body, her gaze falling on Kellan, who lay motionless nearby. The sight of him—so still, so pale—struck her like a knife to the heart. He had sacrificed himself to weaken the beast, and in doing so, had given them a chance to fight. Now, he was paying the price.

She knelt beside him, brushing her fingers across his brow. "I'm sorry," she whispered, her voice thick with grief. Kellan's eyes fluttered open, just barely. A faint smile touched his lips, though it was weak, fading fast.

"There's nothing to be sorry for," he rasped, his voice barely audible. "I knew... what I was doing. It had to be done." His eyes flicked to Damon, who stood silently behind Lyra, his expression solemn.

"You were always braver than any of us gave you credit for," Damon said, his voice soft but firm. "We couldn't have done this without you."

Kellan let out a small, breathless laugh. "That's... good to hear," he murmured, his eyes closing once more. "Take care of each other."

With those final words, Kellan's chest rose and fell one last time, his body going still. Lyra closed her eyes, tears slipping down her cheeks as she leaned into Damon's embrace. They had lost so much, and while the battle was over, the cost was heavy.

The first light of dawn began to creep over the mountains, casting long shadows across the battlefield. The eclipse had passed, and with it, the suffocating darkness that had lingered in the mountains for so long. Lyra stood beside Damon, the two of them staring out at the horizon, knowing that while this chapter of their lives had ended, a new one was just beginning.

The bond between them was gone, but the connection they had forged through love and sacrifice remained. It wasn't the magic that defined them—it was the strength they drew from each other.

"We've faced so much," Lyra whispered, her voice barely louder than the breeze that swept through the valley. "But we're still standing."

Damon squeezed her hand, his thumb tracing small circles on the back of it. "And we'll face whatever comes next," he said, his voice resolute. "Together."

They turned away from the battlefield, from the bodies of the fallen, and began the slow walk back down the mountain. The wind howled softly around them, carrying the distant sound of a lone wolf's howl. It was a reminder that their journey was far from over, that the prophecy still held secrets yet to be revealed.

But for now, they had each other. And no prophecy, no dark magic, could take that away.

Twenty-One

Epilogue: Shadows of Tomorrow

The moon was full, casting a silver glow over the forest. Lyra stood at the edge of the cliff, her eyes scanning the horizon. The wind was crisp, carrying the scent of pine and something else—something darker. Her heartbeat quickened, but she forced herself to breathe slowly. This was supposed to be a moment of peace.

"I thought we agreed no more brooding," Damon's voice broke through her thoughts, soft but teasing.

Lyra turned, a smile pulling at the corner of her lips despite the tension in her chest. "I'm not brooding. I'm… thinking."

"Dangerous." He stepped closer, the heat of him immediately grounding her. Damon always had that effect—calming her when everything else felt uncertain.

"Things are changing," Lyra said quietly, looking back at the dark line of the forest. "I can feel it. Can't you?"

Damon was silent for a moment, his gaze shifting toward the same horizon. "Yeah," he admitted. "I feel it. Something's coming."

Lyra's jaw tightened. The weight of the prophecy hung over them, like a storm cloud that never quite passed. Alaric had been the beginning, but he hadn't been the end. They both knew that.

"Eamon said we'd have time," Damon continued, his tone steady, though Lyra could hear the edge of uncertainty beneath it.

"Eamon also said the prophecy was fulfilled," Lyra shot back. "We know how that turned out."

Damon smirked. "Fair point."

The silence that followed wasn't uncomfortable, but it was charged, like the air before a storm. Lyra wrapped her arms around herself, not from the cold, but from the strange sensation creeping along her skin.

"Do you ever think about what's next?" she asked, her voice soft, almost hesitant.

Damon looked at her, his dark eyes filled with a mix of affection and something more. "With you? Always."

Lyra's smile was small, but genuine. She knew what he meant. They had faced down monsters, magic, and everything in between, but the future—the unknown—that was the real challenge. A life without the bond, without the magic that had once connected them. It was strange, but it felt more real than anything they'd had before.

"We're stronger now," Damon said, as if reading her thoughts. "We don't need the bond to know we belong together."

Lyra nodded, but the unease in her chest didn't fade. "It's not us I'm worried about."

Damon frowned, his gaze sharpening. "What then?"

She hesitated, searching for the right words. "It's just... it's quiet. Too quiet. Ever since Alaric, it feels like we're waiting for the next hit. Like this calm isn't real."

Damon didn't respond immediately. Instead, he stepped forward, standing shoulder to shoulder with her, his eyes fixed on the forest below. "You're not wrong," he said finally. "Something's coming. I don't know what, but we'll be ready."

Lyra exhaled, grateful for his certainty even if she didn't fully share it. She glanced at him, her gaze softening. "We always are."

A rustling sound from behind made them both stiffen. Damon's hand instinctively went to the dagger at his waist, and Lyra's muscles tensed. They turned in unison, their senses sharpening.

A figure emerged from the trees, moving quickly but without urgency. It was Eamon, his face shadowed by the hood of his cloak. He paused when he saw them, his expression unreadable.

"Eamon," Damon greeted, though there was a cautious edge to his voice. "What are you doing here?"

Eamon pulled back his hood, revealing the deep lines etched into his face. He looked older, more weary than before. "We need to talk."

Lyra exchanged a glance with Damon before stepping forward. "What is it?"

Eamon hesitated, his gaze flicking between them. "There's something… stirring. An ancient power. Older than Alaric. Older than the packs."

Lyra's stomach dropped. "What kind of power?"

Eamon's eyes darkened. "The kind that doesn't stay buried."

Damon straightened, his jaw tightening. "How long do we have?"

Eamon shook his head, the grimness in his expression deepening. "Not long. The signs are already here. It's waking."

A chill ran down Lyra's spine. She had felt it—an unsettling shift in the air, a pull toward something she couldn't quite name. Now, hearing it confirmed out loud only made it worse.

"We'll need to gather the others," Damon said, his voice firm. "We'll need to be prepared."

Eamon nodded, his gaze distant. "This isn't like before. It's bigger. More dangerous. We can't face this alone."

Lyra's hands clenched into fists, a fierce determination rising in her chest. She had lost too much already. Whatever this new threat was, it wouldn't take more from her.

"We'll fight," she said, her voice steady despite the fear curling inside her. "We'll fight like we always do."

Damon's hand found hers, a silent promise in his touch. "Together."

Eamon gave a curt nod, then turned back toward the trees. "I'll gather the others. Be ready."

As he disappeared into the darkness, Lyra stood beside Damon, the weight of what was coming pressing down on them both.

"This isn't over," Damon murmured, his eyes still fixed on the place where Eamon had vanished.

Lyra tightened her grip on his hand. "It never is."

They stood there, side by side, staring into the night, waiting for the storm that they knew was coming. And when it did, they would be ready.

www.ingramcontent.com/pod-product-compliance
Ingram Content Group UK Ltd.
Pitfield, Milton Keynes, MK11 3LW, UK
UKHW051343070125
3990UKWH00041B/466